Wesley

Hathaway House, Book 23

Dale Mayer

WESLEY: HATHAWAY HOUSE, BOOK 23
Beverly Dale Mayer
Valley Publishing Ltd.

ISBN-13: 978-1-778860-16-4
Print Edition

Books in This Series:

Aaron, Book 1

Brock, Book 2

Cole, Book 3

Denton, Book 4

Elliot, Book 5

Finn, Book 6

Gregory, Book 7

Heath, Book 8

Iain, Book 9

Jaden, Book 10

Keith, Book 11

Lance, Book 12

Melissa, Book 13

Nash, Book 14

Owen, Book 15

Percy, Book 16

Quinton, Book 17

Ryatt, Book 18

Spencer, Book 19

Timothy, Book 20

Urban, Book 21

Victor, Book 22

Wesley, Book 23

Xavier, Book 24

Boxed Sets and Bundles

https://geni.us/Bundlepage

About This Book

Welcome to Hathaway House. Rehab Center. Safe Haven. Second chance at life and love.

Dealing with the loss of his right leg was one thing, but dealing with his missing left arm was more than Wesley can handle. He can hide the prosthetic leg. However, the arm is damn-near impossible to make look normal. And being normal mattered—or so he thought.

Alba is a therapist at Hathaway House, helping the patients come to terms with their new reality, in order to have the highest-functioning future possible. Wesley is on her roster, but, as their sessions progress, a connection builds that is hard to resist—or to ignore. But she has to stay professional. Yet, when she points out a few issues to help him change his perspective, their friendship hits a rocky spot. Needing to find her balance again, she pulls back.

Only when Wesley accidentally meets a young girl, visiting her father at the center, does Wesley get the paradigm shift he needs. The transformation is there within his reach, if he makes the effort. And the results will be worth it. He knows that. As Alba once again returns to his inner circle, he realizes just how much effort he's willing to put in to get everything he wants.

Sign up to be notified of all Dale's releases here!
https://geni.us/DaleNews

WESLEY BRODEN STARED at the inside of the ambulance. He couldn't believe he had to travel this way. It was a six-hour drive, but he couldn't find anybody else to take him, so this was about the only way to go. It wasn't necessarily a true ambulance. It was more of an interfacility transfer vehicle.

The paramedic looked down at him. "You doing okay?"

He nodded. "Yeah, I'm fine. I had hoped to find somebody with a truck to get me there."

"Not advised," he replied. "Anybody in your condition will find it very painful to go that far for six long hours."

"It *is* much more comfortable to lie down," Wesley admitted.

The paramedic nodded. "That stump of yours is pretty sore, isn't it?"

"Both of them." He nodded. "They were doing better, and then they weren't. I tried to … I wore the prosthetics too much," he shared, hating to admit it. "I just was really happy to get back up and to have some mobility. And then, of course, I pushed it."

"Yeah, that happens," the EMT noted, "especially on your left arm."

"Yeah, I don't have much of a stump." He had about four inches down from the shoulder. "I was really trying hard to make the prosthetic work because I hate not being independent," he said, his tone letting through a tinge of anger.

"And yet there's times when you need help, like all of us." The paramedic lifted his pant leg and showed him his lower leg, which was a prosthetic.

Wesley stared at it. "Well, that gives me hope," he said.

"Don't ever lose hope," the EMT declared. "I lost my leg when I was sixteen in a motorcycle accident, and I thought my life was over at the time," he admitted, "but it's not. It happened long ago, and I survived pretty fast. I had to have surgery and rehabilitation," he added, "but it is what it is. I'm fine with it. My wife's fine with it. My kids think it's cool."

Wesley laughed. "I can see that too. That almost sounds like fun when you're a kid. I'm probably not a whole lot older than you, but, at the moment, I think my arm amputation bothers me more than the leg."

"Of course. At Hathaway," he offered, "you'll do just fine." He pointed out the window. "You can see the grounds just coming up here. I've delivered a couple people here, and every time I think what an absolutely incredible place it is. I've looked it up a couple times, and the reviews and awards it's won are just incredible," he shared. "You're in good hands here."

Wesley nodded. "I hope so. Sometimes you just want to give up."

"Don't give up," the EMT stated. "I'm proof that you can have a life after amputation. Even double amputations," he added. "Find something you want to do with your life and stick with it and don't let anybody tell you differently." And those were definitely words to live by.

"Do you know anybody who works there?" Wesley asked him.

"Several people," he replied. "Dani, the co-owner, I've talked to her a couple times. I've had a friend go through here. She mentioned Dennis in the kitchen—apparently he's quite a character. I don't know anybody else right now, but that doesn't mean a whole lot." As he pointed out the window again, he said, "Look. Somebody is out riding horses."

Wesley shifted so that he could look outside. "Wow, I would love to get back to horseback riding."

"They have training here for the patients too," the EMT offered.

A couple people were out there. Wesley watched the woman, with her long red braid bouncing behind her, as she moved the horses at a great clip.

"Well, if nothing else," the paramedic added, with a big smile, "you'll have lots of good things to look at."

Wesley wasn't sure whether the EMT meant the woman or the horse. But, in truth, the two of them moved as one and looked absolutely stunning. "I used to ride like that," Wesley muttered.

"And you can again," the paramedic vowed. "Don't worry. Have a little faith, and it'll take you a long way."

And, with that, they pulled into the driveway and up to the front of Hathaway House and the new beginning of Wesley's life.

Chapter 1

W ESLEY LOOKED UP at the ceiling of his room and released a slow, relaxing breath. He'd survived his first night at Hathaway. Now, there was both excitement and trepidation as to what was coming. He'd had everything explained to him last night, and that was all fine and dandy, but explanations were not the same thing as reality. He understood there would be a day of rest but also some testing, if they could work that in for today. As long as it was not strenuous, he was okay with it.

As he rested on the hospital bed, he was surprised at how well he'd slept. He hadn't slept well for a long time. Maybe a sign of good things to come. He shifted and reached out for his phone, grateful that he could get it all set up with numbers for his team and got it charged last night. He checked to see several texts from friends, one asking how Hathaway House was and another from his mother, asking how the trip was.

Holding the phone on his lap with his bed now adjusted, so he was sitting a little bit higher, he carefully answered. He was still adjusting to not being able to hold his phone properly, what with one arm and no prosthetic on the other. Right now, he had to lay down the phone and text with his good hand. He could use voice commands but he was just stubborn enough to want to improve his physical abilities that he put up with being slow on his phone for the moment.

It took time, but he answered everybody, while looking up at times to check the view out his window. He could tell that, as much as he didn't want to admit it so much to himself, he was looking to see if that woman he'd seen on his way in was out there riding again. She'd looked so at home on a horse that he figured she had to be somebody who either worked with them all the time or at least got out and rode all the time. Something he would love to do, and seeing her out there had given him hope that that was possible here. Still, he was a long way away from that yet.

He threw back the covers, grabbed his crutch that he kept close by, and hobbled to the bathroom, thankful that his missing arm and his missing leg were on opposite sides. Done with that, he eyed the shower, wondering where his strength level was at but figured that he would be okay, so he went through the process. He wasn't bad at handling some things on his own, but other things he really sucked at.

Yet he was getting better all the time. And seeing his paramedic on the way here with his own prosthetic—and farther down the road than Wesley currently was—had given him something to think about. Of course many veterans and others had a missing leg, but nobody ever seemed to have a missing arm.

However, that wasn't true. He'd certainly met a lot of people who had an arm missing and even some—like him— who had both missing. It seemed easier to blame the circumstances, saying that things were different because he had a unique situation. Yet really everybody was unique. It was all how they utilized what they had.

Wesley wanted to get proficient or better than proficient

at doing without two limbs. And that was a problem. Because, so far, every time he'd tried to get back on his prosthetic leg, he had sored up his stump. The surgeries had put him back under but had built up his leg stump and his arm stump with a thick layer of muscle-bound skin. He had high hopes for both areas now, but he still hadn't been cleared to get back up on his leg prosthetic.

That, he knew, would make a huge difference in his mental outlook. Just something about being vertical was inspiring, but it wouldn't help any for his missing arm, and he knew it. He'd already heard all those platitudes about, *Hey, be grateful you still have one arm, be grateful that it's your left arm that's missing and not your right,* on and on, *blah, blah, blah, blah.* And they always came from people who had two arms.

As much as Wesley understood why they were doing it, it was also hard to listen to that over and over again. He had other things in his life besides that to deal with, but he was working on getting to the point where it didn't bother him as much. He wasn't there yet, and he knew it. But maybe, just maybe, he would get there.

When a knock came at his door, he called out, "Come in." He pulled the sheet up over his stump and hips. He was just wearing his khaki pants. A woman stepped in, and he vaguely remembered her from last night. "Hey." He gave her a smile. "I think your name's Dani."

"Yep, good memory."

He shrugged. "I saw a lot of new faces last night," he admitted, "but I don't remember what your role is."

"That's fine," she replied gently. "I came here to see if you are up for going down for breakfast."

He nodded. "I'm kinda hungry."

"Good." She walked over and pivoted his wheelchair and pushed it toward him. "Let's go. I'm hungry too." When he frowned at her, she shrugged. "I run the place, so I have breakfast here too."

"Oh, right, you're *that* Dani."

"I don't know that there's another Dani here," she teased, "but, yep, I'm definitely *that* Dani."

Flushing and feeling a bit embarrassed that he hadn't remembered that part, he added, "I think I saw you when I first came in yesterday, out with the horses?"

"Yes." She smiled and nodded. "We were out for a ride."

"Yeah, another woman was with you," he noted blithely, "a redhead."

Dani laughed. "Her name's Alba. She works here too."

"Does she?" He looked up at her in surprise.

She nodded. "She's an old friend of mine from high school, and, when an opening came, I convinced her to come."

"And what does she do?"

"She's one of the counselors on board and is just completing her PhD in psychology."

"Interesting. So is that somebody I'll possibly talk with regarding my issues?"

"It's possible," Dani replied. "I would have to see whether she's on your team or not. Is that a problem if she is?" He shook his head, but maybe shook it a little too fast because her grin flashed in his direction. "Glad to hear that. Now, get your butt in here." She pointed at the wheelchair, a big grin on her face.

He threw back the covers, and, with her firmly holding the wheelchair, he hopped over and sat down. He grabbed his T-shirt nearby and pulled it on.

She looked at his empty pant leg. "Do you want it pinned up?"

"No, I generally just roll it, like this." And he showed her as he rolled it and tucked it underneath.

"As long as it's comfortable for you," she noted. Then she stepped behind him and pushed him forward.

"I can roll on my own," he protested.

"You can, but today's a long day of testing for you," she shared. "So today you get the treatment."

"Okay, but, just so you know, I am perfectly capable."

"Glad to hear that," she said cheerfully. "A lot to be ready for today. So just be aware that there will be lots of situations that might throw you off."

"Got it, so, in that case, I'll accept the help gratefully."

"Good. Around here, we encourage everyone to accept all the help offered," she stated.

As they went along the hallway, he asked questions about the various places on the floor.

"Yep, this is an open sitting area for everybody," she murmured. "There's also a pool table, some Ping-Pong tables."

"Ping-Pong." He had to laugh. "My reflexes are not up to that."

"Doesn't mean they won't be soon," she pointed out.

He hesitated, then didn't say anything else.

After a moment she looked at him and asked, "You okay?"

"Yeah." He nodded. "Just this question is in the back of my head, but it seems foolish, so I'm trying to argue with myself about asking it."

"Ask away," Dani urged. "The only stupid question is the one you didn't ask."

He laughed at that. "I guess what I really want to know is, does anybody …" He hesitated again, and then the words came out in a rush. "Does anybody ever fail here?"

"Fail?" she repeated, rolling the word around her tongue. "I don't know that *failure* is really a word that we ever use here. … We have people who do phenomenally well. We have people who do great. We have people who do well. We have had a couple people who returned to the hospital because they'd overdone it, and we have had people who've gone to hospital because other conditions came up, and no way we could fix them here," she explained. "I don't think *failure* is exactly something that I've ever heard used."

"So do you ever send people away because they're not showing progress? Do you send people away because they're too difficult to get along with?" He again paused. "I've heard a lot about this place. The paramedic on the way over had a lot to say, and it was all good and positive, but it's like all those reviews on the big online stores. You read them all, and then you wonder how much people got paid to write them, and you start to get jaded."

"I understand that," she admitted. "It's one of the reasons, when I come to reviews, I tend not to read the one stars. Those are usually people pissed about a product and either didn't do anything to fix it or didn't return it to be replaced or whatever the reason. I usually go to the three-star reviews and see what criticisms people have."

Wesley nodded. "I've done something similar too. But it is a bit of a concern that everybody's got all these glowing reports about Hathaway House. And then you come to the point where you're wondering if you'll match up."

"Meaning that you might be the one person who doesn't make it?" Dani asked, frowning.

He looked over at her. "I guess that sounds foolish, doesn't it?"

"I've heard that worry quite a few times from our patients."

"Really?" he asked, twisting in his seat to look up at her.

"Yes, and glad to see you don't have any back problems."

He looked at her and realized that his mobility told her a lot. "Me too. Generally my back isn't too bad. … The problem has been lack of muscle on the stumps, so they don't interact well with the prosthetics." He tapped his little wing. "This causes me the most trouble."

She nodded. "According to the medical records, it's sored up from use, but it's usable. Is that correct?"

"Yes, but I don't have the strength in the arm to carry anything with it."

"I'm sure Shane can work on that," she mentioned.

"Shane?"

"Your physiotherapist. Well, he's the head of physiotherapy, so you might have somebody else in that department working with you. However, he'll be the one who overlooks the team."

"Ah, and this friend of yours, Alba, what does she do again?"

"She's a counselor," Dani replied.

"Right," he muttered, feeling foolish.

And then suddenly they were at these huge open doors. "Wow, where is this?"

"You're heading into the dining area," she replied. And she pushed him up to a line of people.

"A line-up already," he muttered, shaking his head.

"A lot of people are here," she shared, "and mealtimes are not something most people miss out on."

"Well, that's good news," Wesley noted. "That means the food's at least worth eating."

A huge man at the counter turned his way and replied in a booming voice, "You bet. Everything here is great food." His face was split into this massive smile, going from ear to ear. "And look. Somebody new."

Dani laughed. "Dennis, this is Wesley."

So this was Dennis. Wesley stared up at the man that the paramedic had mentioned and nodded. "I've actually heard about you."

Dennis's eyebrows shot up. "All good things, I hope."

"They were good things," Wesley admitted. "The paramedic who brought me over had heard about you. Somebody he knew worked here. Or maybe he went through as a patient," he added, confused for a moment. He shook his head. "I can't remember, but he mentioned that you were in the kitchen and that really good food was here."

Dennis nodded. "And he is correct. We offer wonderful food here."

Wesley asked, "What do you have today? I see lots of choices."

"We offer foods you would want or need," he began, before reeling off some, "and, if you need more, you come back for seconds, you hear me?"

He looked up at him. "Wow."

Dennis nodded. "We know perfectly well that you need food to heal, and you need good food. So tell me what it will be for now."

"I hate to say it," Wesley replied, "but I think I want all of it."

At that, Dennis's laughter boomed out loud and clear. "And hearing those words is a good thing," he noted.

At that, the woman in front of Wesley turned to smile at him. "Glad to see you have an appetite."

And, sure enough, the beautiful redhead from the horse-back-riding scene stood before him. Wesley went silent.

She looked over at Dani and greeted her. "Hey, Dani. How are you this morning?"

"I'm good. Alba, this is Wesley. He saw us out riding yesterday, when he came in."

"Oh, hey, welcome aboard."

"Thanks. Half the reason why I was so fascinated," he replied, "is I haven't had a chance to ride in quite a few years."

Both of them looked at him with interest.

He shrugged. "I was raised on a farm in Montana. Horseback riding is second nature—or maybe I should say *was* second nature."

"And it will be again," Alba declared, eyeing him with an interested look. "We have a horseback-riding program here for our patients as well. Just say the word, and we'll get you all signed up to it."

"I would love to get back on a horse," Wesley admitted. "I don't know how that would work though."

She looked at his injuries and shrugged. "I think it'll work just fine."

He looked back at Dani, and she nodded. "We run a lot of people through that program, and I can tell you that your injuries are comparable with a lot of what we have dealt with," she shared. "Obviously we'll rope Shane in as part of this discussion, so he can work on ensuring that you have developed the right muscles and strengthened up those muscles to handle the ride."

Wesley nodded. "That sounds good."

And then Dennis placed a full tray of food across his lap.

Wesley stared down at the food. "Oh my God, I think I've died and gone to heaven."

Dennis looked at him. "Were you shorted on food before?"

"I was given a *serving*, but it sure didn't look like this."

Dennis once again gave him a fat smile and nodded. "Welcome aboard. You'll do just fine here."

ALBA LAUGHED AT the look of sheer delight on Wesley's face. "Come on. Let's get you to a table. We're all sitting down to have breakfast too."

"Does the staff all eat here?" he asked.

She shook her head. "No, not all the staff even lives here," she noted, "but, for those of us who do, the food's a godsend." And then she patted her flat stomach. "As long as we keep it in control. Dennis is well-known for lots of food, and good food makes you want to just eat and eat. And, if you ever get a chance to ask for one of his ice creams," she shared, shaking her head, "be aware that what he considers small is monstrous for the rest of us."

"I do like ice cream," Wesley declared, with a happy sigh.

"I heard that," Dennis called back.

Wesley laughed. As he wheeled forward in the line-up, Dani directed him on, while she hung back to get her food. "Keep going straight and come up to the left side," she explained. "We're all heading over to that table over there."

Wesley just followed orders, only to realize that they included him. That was amazing in itself, but maybe they did this for guys on their first day. But he certainly wouldn't argue. First days were bad no matter where you were. And, being here, it looked to be not quite as big a challenge as he had thought.

Dani motioned to the table, as she set down her tray. "Set up your food and get comfortable at the table. I'll go get some coffee. Do you want one?"

He looked at her and nodded. "Thank you, I would really appreciate that."

His instinct was to rush and get it for himself, but obviously everybody here was used to helping everyone out. Which, given the kind of center it was, maybe that made sense—although the center he had just come from was different. Everybody had been a stickler for making sure the patients were independent and didn't become too accustomed to getting help. He wasn't sure if it was a good thing or a bad thing here, but he really appreciated people helping, without having it hammered into his head.

As he slowly unpacked his tray, he studied the food in front of him—sausages and eggs and ham and bacon and hash browns. And he even had a fried tomato. That made his heart warm. It wasn't something he got all that often, but he sure loved them.

Then as he was settled into place, Alba joined him, placing her tray down with about one-third of the food that Wesley had been given. He stared at her. "So how come I look like I'm a pig compared to your plate?" And then he pointed at Dani's and added, "She's even eating more than you."

"Because I'll come back for cinnamon buns in a couple hours," she shared, with an equally fat smile.

"Just the look on your face says a lot," Wesley noted.

"It's an odd thing here to have so much help offered, and obviously I'll adjust. However, in my last center, everybody was a stickler on being independent, and, if you can do it yourself, you shouldn't accept any help," he explained, with a wave of his hand. "And yet you guys all seem to be totally okay to help."

"Sure," she agreed. "You have enough tough times ahead of you in physio," she noted, "and, even today, it could be tough with testing. So we're not trying to stress you out. Therefore, if we can help, it's good for us to remember to offer," she shared, with a smile. "It would be nice if more people helped. After all, you are here for rehab, and it's a strenuous program. You'll be home soon enough and on your own, where you have to do everything. So I understand the need to foster independence," she admitted, "but there's also a time when it's just offered to be nice, to make some-one else's day a little better."

He nodded. "And I appreciate that," he murmured. "Thank you."

She laughed. "You're more than welcome. You'll find most of us here are friendly."

"Oh, I'm certainly seeing that," Wesley replied, with a smile. "And that's really good to see."

She looked over at him. "Sounds as if you've had a hard time at the other place."

"I didn't realize I had, at the time," he shared. "Yet you never really know sometimes, not unless you get to compare it to another way."

"That's true," she agreed. "Sometimes what you think works doesn't necessarily work. You had just hoped that it did."

He looked at her and then nodded slowly. "I think that

is very true. And just because you hoped it worked doesn't mean you can make a square peg fit into a round hole."

"Exactly," she murmured. She watched him, seeing that he was still hesitating before starting in on his food. "Go ahead and eat," she urged.

"I was thinking I should wait for Dani. She's been nice enough to come and find me and to ensure I came here and got food, so I feel bad to not wait for her."

"Go for it," Alba insisted, as she picked up her fork. "Around here, waiting is not really an option. Most of us are on schedules of one kind or another, as you'll soon find out when your own fills up," she explained, "so Dani would certainly understand."

He hesitated and realized that Alba was eating and nodded. "Okay, but I'll just go on record here and say that I tried."

"You tried what?" Dani asked, as she appeared suddenly, setting down coffee cups for them all.

"I tried to wait for you," he murmured, "but Alba here is insistent that I don't need to wait."

"Oh my, you definitely do not need to wait."

"See? I told you," Alba noted, with a laugh.

He just grinned and shook his head. "That's fine. I just didn't want Dani to think I was being rude."

"And I wouldn't think that anyway," Dani murmured, still standing. "You eat, as you'll have a day of testing and all kinds of fun stuff, so go ahead and get started."

"Won't you join us?" he asked, pointing at her plate, sitting there and waiting.

"Oh, I'm coming back," she replied, with a laugh. "I just have more pieces to collect."

He watched her as she headed back over again. He

looked over at Alba.

Alba nodded. "She's probably just getting water now."

"You mentioned something about cinnamon buns earlier."

At that, Alba looked back at Dani and then stood up to peer toward the kitchen area. "If she's getting cinnamon buns, you should pay attention because she has, I swear, a direct line to them."

"Well, if she runs this place," Wesley pointed out, with a laugh, "she probably does."

"Agreed, and with good reason. She works harder than any of us. She's done so much for everyone here."

"I have heard various tidbits about her, but she's not what I expected."

At that, Alba raised her eyebrows.

"Well, she's like thirty years younger than what I thought," he admitted, with a smile. "And she's way prettier."

At that, Alba laughed out loud. "She is taken too."

"Of course she is," he muttered, with an eye roll. "All the good ones are."

"Oh no, no, no, no," Alba countered, with a laugh. "I'm not taken, and I refuse to think that I'm not one of the good ones."

He flushed at that. "Sorry, I guess that didn't come across all that nice, did it?"

"That's okay. You're forgiven," she replied. "Just remember that we're not all taken. And I'm still a nice person."

He chuckled. "And you're beautiful, so I'm not sure what's wrong with the men in this place that you're not taken."

"When I got here, it wasn't a priority. I was trying to fit in, to settle in, and to find a clear path in my field to help everybody here," she shared, with a smile. "And, since then, I just haven't met anybody."

"I still think the men here are missing out on something major," he declared, staring at her. "Seems to me you've got your life together."

"But what do you know?" she teased. "You just got here. It could all be an act."

"Absolutely," he agreed, "but being the new guy also means that I can see what other people aren't seeing," he pointed out. "And obviously the men around here are blind."

She flushed with pleasure and then laughed out loud. "I'll have to watch out for that smooth tongue of yours," she said, still chuckling.

At that moment Dani returned but without a cinnamon bun.

Alba eyed her friend suspiciously and said, "If you get a line on those cinnamon buns today …"

"Yep, yep, yep, I know," Dani replied, "you want one."

"Yeah, I definitely want one."

"So do I," Wesley chimed in. "I'm not sure what I'm missing out on, but I'm really not into missing out on very much."

At that, Dani chuckled. "Maybe you don't like cinnamon buns."

He frowned at her. "Is that even a possibility?" he asked. "Doesn't everyone love cinnamon buns?"

"Lots of people don't love them," she stated firmly. "However, I do. And don't worry. They're coming out in a couple hours."

"So today will be cinnamon bun day," Alba noted, rubbing her hands together. Then she laughed with joy. "So today will be a good day after all."

Chapter 2

NOT ONLY WAS it a good day, but Alba got a cinnamon bun herself, before they were all gone. However, it did take Dani's reminder for Alba to get up away from her desk and to follow her friend to the kitchen. "I don't understand why we can't just get Dennis to set them off to the side for us," she complained good-naturedly.

"Could be because Dennis is a little on the busy side," he stated, hearing her words.

She laughed. "Right? And, if you were on cinnamon bun duty, you would have to make so many because everybody would then want them delivered."

"Oh, you're not kidding," he muttered. "Can you imagine what my life would be like if I only delivered to some people?"

She nodded. "You can get away with it for Dani though."

"Sure, Dani's the boss, and she deserves delivery." He looked at Alba pointedly and said, "Yet you, on the other hand ..."

At that she burst out laughing. "Right, message received," she replied, still chuckling.

"You know that you can come get one anytime you want one."

"That only works," she murmured, "if I'm on time for

getting them."

He nodded. "Good point. ... Still, it's up to you to ensure you're here before the crowd."

She sighed. "Which just means that I get one out of every four times that they come out," she shared, "because, if anybody is five minutes late, they're gone."

He handed her a plate with a big one on it. "This'll help make up for some of those other days."

She looked down at it in fascination. "I don't know how you guys make them so good," she murmured. "I have tried an endless number of times, and I just never quite get that same flavor."

"It's Ilse's family recipe," he noted, with a chuckle. "Not sure she's up for passing it along either."

"No, she probably isn't, and you can't really blame her," Dani added. "Some of these recipes, we have been blessed to have here," she stated, with a smile.

"If you ever needed to make some money—and Ilse too," Alba suggested, "convince Ilse to share some of the recipes and publish a cookbook because an awful lot of people absolutely love her food here."

"And that's not a bad idea," she replied thoughtfully. "Something else to think about down the road. I certainly can't do anything about it right now."

"Of course not," Alba agreed. "Like the rest of us, we're all just so busy. And it never gets any easier," she noted. "Hathaway is a busy place, and it stays busy."

"Yeah, it does, even when we think it'll be an easier day," Dani said, with a smile.

"And yet it's never quite that easy," Alba pointed out, laughing. Then she asked, "How's the new guy adjusting?"

"You can ask him yourself," Dani stated. "He's on your

roster."

"Is he? Interesting."

"And is that a note of interest?" Dani asked curiously, looking over at Alba.

"Hey, he was interesting to get to know at breakfast this morning," she replied. "He seemed a little flabbergasted at all the food and just the way the place operates."

"I've heard that a few times. Everybody has their own system and how they make things work," Dani noted. "So it's a little frustrating when they come here with such low expectations, expecting poor food, small servings, and to be treated indifferently. Yet they generally adapt very quickly."

"Oh, I think he'll adapt just fine," Alba declared. "He was working on it pretty fast this morning."

"I think he was just working on breakfast this morning, afraid some of it would disappear."

"Do you think he really did just get portioned-out food?"

"Lots of places do it that way," Dani murmured. "I've always held the belief that it was more important for people to enjoy their food and to be happy and that having good food was a good way to make them happy and healthier too," she explained. "And thankfully, Ilse has always agreed with me."

"You're right," Alba agreed, "particularly people who have a lot of challenges."

"Exactly, but, for a lot of them, they see those challenges as something they'll have to get over, and they might as well just start now," she murmured. "And that can make for a few other challenges."

ALBA WALKED INTO work the next morning, she came upon Wesley, as he navigated through the hallway. "Are you lost?" she called out to him.

He turned and flashed her a shy smile. "Yes," he admitted, holding up his e-tablet. "I know there's a map of this place, but honestly it's a little confusing."

She nodded. "The new patient wing has added to the confusion. Where are you heading?"

He looked down at his device. "To Dr. Fendrick."

"You're in luck. That's me."

He frowned at her. "I guess I didn't catch your last name yesterday. Sorry."

"Not an issue," she said. "Come on with me. My office is down here. You're a little early."

"I figured early would allow me time to find the place," he shared. "I wasn't expecting to run into you here."

"I'm all over the place," she murmured.

"And how long have you been here?" he asked.

"Ah, four years now, I think," she replied, looking at him with a smile. "Any other questions?"

"I'm sure there'll be lots. However, after you've had a number of people on your supposed support team," he shared, "it makes you a little leery of some."

She looked at him. "Well, you're welcome to ask any questions you want. Absolutely no reason you can't ask questions of me, since I ask them of you."

"That's good to know."

And she could see from his surprise that he hadn't expected that. She smiled at him. "No secrets here. We're all on the same team, trying to get you back on your feet as quickly as possible."

"Yeah," he agreed, "at least back on one, and I really

want to find a way to make the arm work better."

She looked at the stump that he had and nodded. "I have seen some people with a shoulder harness to help support the prosthetic arm and fingers, while the muscles in your arm are built up more."

He nodded. "Yeah, I had one, but it kept soring up the stump," he said. "We ended up taking it off. They're supposed to be modifying my leg prosthetic too, maybe making it lighter in weight. Maybe we'll go with a completely different design. Every time I wear either of them, I end up taking them off and then find myself held back by weeks."

"Then definitely don't wear those," she said. "Be sure to mention any concerns you have with Shane, and he will work on getting you a new model."

"That's what I was hoping," Wesley said. "I didn't want to upset the guys who had been working on it before, but I'm no longer in the same hospital either."

"And I don't know how that works," she noted. "Something for us to look into."

"Or maybe I can get new ones?" he asked hopefully.

She shrugged. "Not my department, but I can put down a note, and we'll see how it goes." She looked at the flap of flesh on his stump. "Did you just have recent surgery?"

"I don't know about *recent* but three months ago."

"That's pretty recent," she replied, "and any prosthetic shouldn't be worn for probably twice that."

"I was a little eager," Wesley admitted, with a nod. "And, yep, my own worst enemy."

As she unlocked her office and pushed open the door, she shared, "News flash, we're all our own worst enemies."

"Oh, it's not an isolated incident then, *huh*? I'm

crushed," he announced. "I was hoping to be special."

She burst out laughing. "We're all special in our own way," she declared. "The joy is in finding it, and the challenge is in letting it come out."

And those were words to live by, and they stuck with her for quite a while. She thought about him long after the session was over. Of course he would be on her roster. She was taking most of the new patients just because her schedule wasn't as busy as some of the longer-term counselors here.

As she went to lunch later, she caught up with Shane. "Hey, have you met up with Wesley yet?"

"Yep, saw him this morning," he said. "Concerns?"

"No, not necessarily," Alba began. "We're just starting obviously, but I was thinking about whether we could get a prosthetic hooked up for that arm of his. He's only three months out of surgery and has pushed it, so then I think whatever he did use wouldn't be viable any longer."

"I'll contact his former center and see if they've got anything. Some of his files came, and some of them look to still be missing," Shane noted. "However, I did see a few notations in there how his prosthetics were hurting him more than helping him."

"And I think that's a huge issue for him."

"As much as covering it up, or just making it viable?"

"Both," she answered. "We all want to look normal, but I think, in his case, it's more a functionality issue than anything. He wants to be vertical, of course, plus he really misses that lost arm. So anything we can do to make his prosthetics more functional is, as you know, obviously a priority."

He nodded. "He also needs a new prosthetic for that leg too."

"Wasn't that some recent surgery too?"

"I'll have to check his file for sure. I think his leg prosthetic is ill-fitting, and he's got some nerve damage on the underside of his stump, so he didn't recognize this problem because it was out of his line of sight. Plus the nerve damage doesn't send the pain signal when there is a problem. Thus he ended up with a bad skin infection. That's slowly healing, but he'll be a little while getting back to his leg prosthetic."

"Right," Alba noted. "It seems to always be one step forward and then ten back."

"Particularly when he couldn't see it himself and couldn't feel it because of the nerve damage. And that's always tough."

She nodded. "I used to work with a family whose ten-year-old son got run over by the mother. It was a horrible accident," she muttered, with a wave of her hand. "It left the boy paralyzed, and he was forever breaking his legs because the pain didn't register. They had no idea because he didn't know how to tell them. Regardless, he must have been active, breaking his legs over and over, so in a constant state of trying to heal."

"God," Shane muttered, "things like that just make me heartsick."

She nodded. "He struggled a lot. As he got a little older and more capable of looking after himself a little bit better, it became easier."

"Easier but still hard," Shane noted, "especially when your own family member caused it."

Alba nodded, grimacing. It had been an awful accident, and she felt for both the mother and the son because there was no good answer for either party in that situation.

As they walked into the dining area, she smiled and said,

"Dani's done a wonderful job with that new kitchen addition."

Shane nodded. "It's taken us a little bit to integrate it with the proper employees, though. We could use more staff."

"Always," she agreed, with a laugh.

They both stepped into line, and she smiled up at Dennis. "Hey, Dennis. How are you doing today?"

"I am doing peachy," he replied, showing her a beaming smile.

"You have got to be the *happiest go-lucky* person I've ever met."

"And maybe it's all a front," he muttered in a dark whisper. "Maybe I'm really a serial killer."

"*Yeah*, you couldn't be a successful serial killer, as you would probably get your prey to laugh and then apologize to everybody afterward for having *bad thoughts*."

He burst out laughing at that. "I'm all about helping my fellow man. You know that."

"And that's why you do so well here," she murmured. "You're in the same mind-set as the rest of us."

"And now that we have that many more patients," he noted, "we are struggling to sort out the food."

"Shane and I were just talking about how we needed more kitchen staff."

"We do have two more kitchen helpers coming," he murmured. "So that will help here."

"And twenty to go overall," Shane added in a dark tone, but then he laughed. "Yet we'll make it, as we always do."

At that, they both grabbed their lunches and headed off to a table. As she walked out onto the deck with Shane at her side, she asked, "Inside or outside?"

"Outside, before it gets too hot," he decided. Then he pointed over to one because, sure enough, Wesley sat all alone.

She nodded. "Hey, Wesley. Do you mind if we join you?"

He looked up, pleased. "I would appreciate it. It's hard being the only man sitting at a table. You start to wonder if everybody's avoiding you."

"*Nah*. You're just the new guy, finding your way. You'll be among many friends soon."

He nodded. "Been the new guy a couple times now. It still sucks."

She looked at him and then nodded. He was serious. "Did you really notice much of the new guy syndrome in the other centers?"

"Yes," he stated, "there was always a little bit of it. A lot of times people hated being there, so a new guy was a change of scenery, a distraction, a good thing in a way. But sometimes there were issues, a little bit of a hierarchy going on, and a new guy had to find a spot to fit in." He shrugged. "As much as I'm okay to fit in, I don't go out of my way."

"And why is that?" she asked, unable to help herself as a counselor.

"Because, when you try to fit in," he explained, "you're always the one who's giving. It's really important for people to establish who they are right from the beginning, not going out of their way to be jerks, but also not to cross the line so that other people can take advantage."

Shane nodded. "That's an interesting take on the world."

"It's a take based on being in the navy and boarding schools before that," Wesley shared. "And the various VA centers, although different, were still very much the same."

Not a whole lot anybody could say at that point, and they all tucked into their lunch.

Wesley lifted his head for air. "Is the food always this good?"

"Always," they both replied in unison.

Wesley grinned. "In that case, I have died and gone to heaven. I didn't know there would be soup today," he shared. "Yet that curiosity alone had me asking for it, and it's absolutely divine."

"It's a beef and barley soup with an Ilse twist, so it's probably got kale and other healthy stuff in it," Shane noted. "Anything to make it healing and to get more vegetables down you."

"I like my vegetables just fine," Wesley stated, "but I have to admit the soup is really good."

"So where are you off to after this?" Alba asked.

"Medical doctor, medical records, *blah, blah, blah, blah.*" He looked over at Shane. "I get that we have some testing still to do, but when do we actually buckle down and get some work done?"

"It'll be this week," he replied comfortably. "What is it you want to start with?"

He lifted his floppy arm and said, "This one."

"And what do you want to do with it?"

"I want to make it strong and, at a maximum, usable," he replied. "I do not know what that means. I'm still missing an arm, so there are obviously limitations, but is there anything I can do to make it usable? Can I get strong enough that I can, I don't know, even pack a book or my e-tablet or something under there?"

"You can't now?" Shane asked, studying his arm.

Wesley shook his head, tucked a napkin underneath, and replied, "I can't close it tight enough," as the napkin fell to the floor.

"What about something bigger, like a towel?"

"I can hook it in there," he replied, "with my good hand, but I still can't keep a lock on it enough with my floppy arm to hold something there."

"Yep, we can definitely start with that arm," Shane declared, studying the stump up to the shoulder joint. "Good thing you mentioned it. I probably would have started with the leg."

"The legs are great, once I have the prosthetic on," he shared. "I can get around, and I can stand vertical and can get that whole *I'm a healthy adult male* vibe again, but the arm is what makes me feel handicapped, and I don't like that."

WESLEY REALLY ENJOYED lunch, but he also really enjoyed the inclusiveness of it. He didn't feel as if he were the odd man out, although he was half-expecting that new man syndrome. Still, he knew the new guy stigma would still be here to a certain extent, but Shane and Alba had both gone out of their way to make Wesley feel welcome. And he was grateful that Shane appeared to be open to listening to what Wesley wanted to work on. That was also a relatively unusual thing in Wesley's world. Everybody seemed to always have an idea of what needed to be done, and nobody ever asked him for an opinion on what he should be doing or what he wanted to do. So this Hathaway House approach gave him hope.

Several days later, Wesley rolled into a session with Shane.

He held up an odd contraption in his hand and announced, "We'll work on this today."

"And what is that?" Wesley asked.

"For strengthening the various arm muscles," Shane replied. "So, consider how we would work with the upper arm and the traps at the gym. This contraption goes about it a little bit differently."

As Shane explained it, Wesley realized that would help him use his floppy arm to push forward, to pull back, to stretch, as in raising and lowering it. The contraption was a series of weights that he would start with to try and clench under his floppy arm. And, of course, his first attempt was a complete and dismal failure. He shook his head as he watched everything fall to the floor time and time again. "Dang it," he muttered.

"It's not a case of failure. It's a case of *this is where we start*, so recognize it as your beginning point and go on from here. Everybody has a bottom level, and this is your bottom level, your starting point, for that arm."

And, with that mind-set, Wesley grimly tucked into trying to build up his floppy arm a little bit. He could do some of the *pull forward* muscles, which he could see would be helpful if he ever had something attached to that arm that he could pull with. However, right now, it seemed to be just one of those useless motions.

But Shane wouldn't listen to him when he mentioned that. "No," he countered. "You can't think in terms of the arm only doing one motion. It has to work as a unit in order to maintain long-term function. It might give you some short-term results, but what you'll end up with are long-term problems that won't be consistent." He added, "You want this long-term, I presume."

"Yeah, of course," Wesley replied. "Are you seriously telling me that it'll hurt to focus on being able to clench more?"

"Yes," Shane confirmed. "It's very important to do it in balance. Think of muscles as generally being paired off, but it's broader than that. If this muscle gets too big, then this one will overcompensate, and it will stop these others from working," he explained. "So we can't have that. You need it all."

Then Shane made Wesley go through the whole range of exercises again. By the time he was done, Wesley was just angry. Angry at the lack of an arm, angry at the part of the arm he still had, angry at what was left for muscles, and, yeah, he had to admit it, angry at himself for not doing better. Plus he was kind of pissed at Shane for showing him just how bad that floppy arm really was. "When I only looked at it for not being able to clench something," he admitted, "it didn't seem all that bad."

"That's because you were linear in your thinking again," Shane pointed out, "and you can't be. I promise, when we get you there, you'll do all sorts of things with it."

He stared at him for a long moment.

Shane flashed him a grin. "Go talk to any of the guys around here—preferably ones who have been here for a little while, who are further along the rehab track," he added, with an eye roll. "And they will tell you that I'm right. We have our methods, and the reason we stick to them is because they work, and anytime we take a shortcut, or we let somebody else take a shortcut," he noted, "there's a problem."

Wesley thought about that later at dinnertime, when he

was sitting at a table with a whole group of guys. He had rolled past them, when somebody had called out and suggested, "Hey, a spot's here if you want." After introductions and a little bit of sharing brief backgrounds, Wesley began, "So Shane has a few interesting techniques."

At that, the others started to laugh.

"Yeah, he does. He's also won multiple awards for his work," one of the men shared. "Took me a long time to believe him. I thought he was full of horsepucky and told him so, over and over again."

Wesley stared at him in fascination. He was a huge guy, missing both legs, just stumps that didn't even reach the end of the wheelchair, plus he was missing his right arm. "And?"

"It took me a while, took me a lot of faith, to follow through on everything he told me," he admitted. "Now? This arm?" he indicated, as he lifted what he had for a stump, which went just past the elbow, "is now strong enough to do things. I have multiple prosthetics, one with a hand, one with a hook. The kids love that one," he muttered. "And one with a cup, where I can carry things around."

"And what about the legs?" asked one of the other guys.

"I've only been here working with Shane for about a month now," he pointed out. "And I haven't seen the progress I want yet."

"And that's probably because you're trying to jump ahead or you see somebody who's doing better, and you want to be that person," interjected the guy whose name was Jim. "And that won't be the way to do it. It takes as long as it takes. Plus, Shane's got some very specific reasons for what he does. Trust a little bit."

At that, Wesley nodded. "Well, I just got here, so I

won't judge until I get further down the line."

"You're already judging," Jim pointed out, with a grin. "And that's to be expected. You probably came from all kinds of other centers, where you were told you could do this or you could do that, or, hey, this might work, that might work. At the end of the day, when nothing worked, you're depressed and fed up."

That was so close to the truth that Wesley just stared at him in shock.

Jim nodded. "Believe me when I say that most of us have been there. Most of us came from somewhere else to be here. Very few of us got in here right off the bat, without having a lot of prejudiced and judgmental thinking before we got here. Most of us, and I don't even know why," he admitted, "but, for a lot of us, this became a last-ditch place. The last place where, maybe, if there was a miracle in the world, we would find it here."

Wesley sat back and stared.

Jim nodded. "I've been here for six months because I came as a basket case, on a stretcher, and I couldn't even sit up. Yet you can see me now. Also I can play basketball. I can be outside, participating in sports." He added, "I really suck at tennis, but I'm getting better every day."

"Tennis?" Wesley asked, staring at him.

"Yeah, tennis. The problem is, as fast as I am, I'm still not quite that fast, if somebody wants to get, you know, really mean."

"You mean, for example, give you a serve that you can't return?"

"Right. So far we're playing nice," he shared. "Then, every once in a while, I play a *real* game, and I get my butt *whupped*," he declared cheerfully. "But sometimes the *butt-*

whupping is a whole lot less than the time before, and I can see that there's real progress yet again. When I didn't think there could be any more progress, I continue to surprise myself at how much better I'm doing."

"How much longer will you be here?" Wesley asked him.

"I'm going home next week," he shared, his face lighting up. "And, man, am I ready to go home. Even though the food's this good, I've got twin boys, who are four years old, and they want, … they want Daddy's hook back," he said, laughing out loud. "And believe me that I just want to go home again to my wife."

"Hey," Wesley added, with feeling, "if you've got family to go to, all the best for you, man. Obviously this place has been a godsend for you."

And it will be for you too," Jim declared. "Seriously, just give it a chance."

Chapter 3

WHEN ALBA WALKED into her office a week later, Wesley was already sitting here, waiting for her. "You are, by far, the most eager person I've ever had in one of my sessions," she stated, staring at him.

"You make it sound like it's a bad thing."

"No, it's not a bad thing," she clarified. "It's just an unusual thing. Sometimes I have to actually hunt down my next patient and bring people down here to talk to me," she admitted, with a grin.

"That's those guys who don't want to face their inner demons," he noted, with a nod.

"And, of course, you've already faced yours, is that it?" she asked, a knowing look in her eyes.

"Nope, but I also know that, when it's time to face them, you must face them, and there's really no getting away from it. So you still won't find me running away from you. Besides, I like you."

And there was such an honesty and an openness about his comment that she was again surprised. "Thank you," she replied. "I like you too."

"So does that mean we can have lunch one day?"

She stopped and turned and asked, "Are you asking me out for a date?" She wasn't shocked, but she was definitely amused.

"I guess I'm not the first one, *huh?*"

"Nope, you're sure not," she said. "At one point in time we didn't allow any dating of the patients, but that's all changed."

"Why is it changed?"

"Well, with Dani herself, as her fiancé was a patient here. And, after you date a patient yourself, it's pretty hard to expect your staff to follow different rules."

He nodded. "So you evaded the question."

"I didn't evade the question," she corrected. "I just haven't answered you yet."

"So I'll take that as a no then for right now. That's okay. I'll ask again."

"And why would you ask again?"

"Down the road, when you know me better," he said, "you're going to love me."

"Wow." She smiled. "Such confidence."

"No, not necessarily confidence," Wesley countered, "but, being in this place, it can give you hope, and it can change your priorities."

"That's true," she agreed. "Have you made any friends?"

"I really connected with Jim, but he just left."

"Jim is a pistol. I don't know if you saw his sons running around the place earlier, with a pair of baby squirrels."

"Baby squirrels?" He stared at her.

"Oh, have you not met Stan in the vet clinic?"

He slowly shook his head. "Nope, I'll say no to that one. I have seen a few animals around, and I was wondering what that was all about."

"Downstairs is an animal clinic, with an awful lot of animals, therapy animals even, that come up to us to help us heal, and we're, at all times, welcome to go down to help

Stan with them."

"Help him how?"

"The animals need love too," she said. "We have several dogs and a couple cats around here that are basically residents, and the only rules really are that you don't get to lock them in your rooms and that you can't ever feed them. Most are on special diets, and some have bodies just like the rest of you guys."

Wesley frowned. "I'll have to go look for those. I can't believe I've been here a whole week, and I didn't realize you are healing animals too."

She nodded. "There's a lot of things to understand about the place."

"I did see the pool. And I told Shane how I wanted to get in there as soon as possible."

"What did Shane say?"

"He was all for it but still said it would be a week."

"That's because he wants to see just what you can do first," she explained.

He nodded. "And, of course, he doesn't know exactly what I can do. So from his perspective it's just the smart answer."

"Of course it is. We don't want anybody to have an accident. And I know you would never do this," she said, her bright grin breaking free, "but some people overexaggerate their abilities."

He nodded. "Same thing happens, no matter where you are," he murmured. "However, I do swim." And then he stopped, looked down at his floppy arm, frowned, and corrected himself. "I used to swim. I have no idea what I'll look like now swimming."

"Is it the looks that bothers you?" she asked him.

"The arm bothers me at all times," he admitted, "and that's just one of those sad realities that I have to deal with."

"And why does it bother you?"

"I think because it makes me look visibly handicapped. It brings stares, brings a lot of attention that I don't like. The wheelchair does not, to the same extent. I think people are more acclimated to seeing wheelchairs or scooters or whatever. However, when you have an arm that looks like this, I think it attracts a lot more attention."

"And you don't like attracting attention?"

He shook his head. "Nope, I sure don't. I would rather be the quiet, silent type in the back of the classroom."

At that, she gave him a knowing look. "I don't think you were ever the shy, retiring type in the back of the classroom. I think you were always the one joking around, making others feel better."

"That's an interesting evaluation, Doc," he noted, almost instinctively sliding back and putting his hand in his pocket.

She smiled at that. "You have a different outlook?"

"No, you're probably right," he admitted, "but, if I did it, it was because I didn't like to see other people who were usually made uncomfortable by some people in the classroom."

"And sometimes you would have staved it off before it ever got there. Thus it became just a modus operandi for you—something that you could do right out of the gate when somebody came along, or when you were in an unusual situation. Not only did it make others feel better, but it made you feel better."

"Got me all figured out, do you?" He gave her a flat stare.

"No," she replied, "not at all, but that's what you're here for. For *you* to figure out. No, not at all," she repeated. "That's for you to figure out. I'm just here to help direct you."

"Well then, maybe direct me into being more comfortable with this arm," he suggested, "because I can see that's something I'll have to live with."

"It is, indeed. Even with a prosthetic on, that arm won't look the same."

"Nope." He grinned though. "I was thinking a Terminator kind of arm would be cool."

"And it would be cool," she agreed, "and a prototype like that is possible, but it takes money. And I mean some serious money."

He nodded. "Ever since I found out about my arm, I've been hunting the internet, looking for gifted designers, wondering just what was out there that I could feel better about wearing."

"And?"

"I found a woman in New Mexico. Kat somebody or other. I might contact her."

"I do know her—know of her," Alba shared. "More than a couple people here have gotten stuff from her."

"I imagine it's pretty amazing, and some of her designs are pretty specific. Of course she's also missing a leg, so, if you're somebody who's utilizing your own tools, I am sure that helps."

"I think it does help," Alba agreed. "Plus I imagine, just even being in that field, that you're there because you love it. And, when you love something, it's easy to work at it until you're really good at it. Is there something that you're really good at?"

"You mean now?" he asked. "No. I used to think I was really good at some things, but I don't know if they're possible anymore."

"Some things like what?"

"You already know about the horseback riding and swimming. Woodworking too. I made my brother and his wife a cradle for their daughter, when she was born," he shared. "Sometimes I look at it, and I wonder if it's even possible to go back to that."

"And yet you have one good arm," she pointed out.

"Yes, and, to a certain extent, that's partly why I want to get the second arm up and running properly," he said. "Just to hold the wood in place, to lift boards, to hold them against table saws, things like that, two hands would be much better."

"Much better, yes," she noted, "but, if you can find a way to make it work without that, you might be able to do it just as well. It will all take adaptation."

"I get that, but, if I can get as far down this pathway as I can," he noted, "there's a lot less adaptation. And I already have to get back and relearn certain things."

"Like what?" she asked curiously.

"Standing, walking, bending, crouching—movements that I took for granted before, which I can't do as easily now. Just because, when woodworking, I would naturally squat and eyeball a line," he explained. "That won't be so easy anymore."

"No, it won't be easy, and you're right. Again it'll take some adjusting. However, it's definitely all within the realm of possibility."

He smiled. "You're definitely a glass-half-full person, aren't you?"

"I am, but you're not a glass-half-empty guy," she pointed out. "You're just sitting there, waffling in the middle, wondering where you belong."

WESLEY STARED AT her in shock. "Wow, more insights."

"Am I correct?"

"Maybe," he murmured. "I hadn't really considered that."

"Well, consider it," she said. "You can go either way. You can be somebody who takes what you got, maximizes it to unbelievable levels, and makes everybody else in the world jealous; or you can stay in that supposed shy retiring back seat that you think you are sitting at, and you can let the world pass you by because you don't think you can get good enough to go back to doing things."

"I can get good enough to go back to doing things," he declared. "I just don't know if I can ever achieve the same level I had before."

"Don't even think about having the same level," she said. "Strive for so much better. Go beyond that. Go to something that's absolutely stupendously advanced. And you might surprise yourself."

THROUGHOUT THE NEXT few days, Wesley understood that Alba was just doing her job, giving him inspirational lines to live by. However, he had to admit that, as her words stuck with him for days afterward, she was really good at her job. He only saw her once a week, and sometimes he thought that wasn't enough. At other times, like now, when he was thinking about the words that she'd dropped on him, it was too much because definitely some core truths were in there that he didn't really want to think about.

Yet she wouldn't let him sit back and be that shy, retiring type he wanted to play. She was right. It was a role, something that he tried to do to make uncomfortable situations easier for him. And then, when he was comfortable, he stepped forward and became his natural normal self. Often some of his friends had mentioned that it was such a contrast to actually get to know him, as he was so different now than how he'd initially appeared. Wesley knew why, and he just didn't want to share how uncomfortable he'd been to begin with.

AS WESLEY WORKED his way through the days, he found himself getting more and more tired. He mentioned it to Shane.

Shane nodded. "You have that initial flush of *Hey, I'm here. It's all new. It's all different. It's all great,*" he explained. "And then you have that *buckle in and get the work done* stage. Afterward you have that realization where the work will still be there, even if you can't complete it, and nobody else can complete it but you. When you're the only person at a job, and you leave something to do, it'll still be there waiting for you the next day because you don't have other employees to pick up the slack. That's what this rehab work is like," Shane declared.

"There are *no* other employees to pick up the slack. This is just on you, you, and you," he said. "So, if you don't do it today, it must be done tomorrow. And, if you don't push yourself today, then you're just adding extra tomorrows to your workload. ... So, once you start in on this path, a certain level of fatigue settles in, when the realization hits you that this is all about hard work."

"I had a lot of hard work at the other place," Wesley argued.

"Sure, so then why are you working so much harder now?"

"Am I?" he asked, studying Shane.

"I would say so. Look at how much progress we've already made."

And the problem with that was, Shane was right. They had made a lot of progress, and Wesley was so happy to see it. Yet he was a long way from where he wanted to be. Still, there had certainly been progress. He could at least now hold a napkin under his little wing. He stared at it. "I wouldn't mind getting into designing stuff like this," he muttered.

"It's quite a specialized field, but an awful lot of people started in their own garage, before they built up to something much bigger and better," Shane noted calmly. "I won't ever tell anybody to not go down a chosen pathway. I'm all for it, even if the pathway doesn't turn out to be profitable or where you want to be. Still, you will learn a lot about yourself in the process." And, with that, Shane asked, "Now, how about the pool?"

Wesley looked at him in shock and then in delight. "Seriously? You're not teasing me today, right?"

Shane laughed. "Nope, I think it's time we go see how you'll do in the pool. Some of the muscles that you need will be ones that we work on in the water," he explained. "So go get changed, and I'll meet you down there"—and he looked at his watch—"in say, fifteen?"

"Sure," Wesley replied. "I guess I can't go into the pool without you, can I?"

"Nope, you sure can't. You wait for me," Shane cautioned. "Not only are there all the lovely little injuries that you could get by having an accident, there's all those lovely liabilities that get us into trouble if we don't follow the book." And, with that, Shane added, "Go. You're on the clock."

Wesley settled into his wheelchair and made his way to his room. He was tired. He was already tired. The thought of going in the pool was almost euphoric. Yet he figured that he would also have to do some work, but it would be a different kind of workout—at least that's what he told himself. With some trepidation, he headed to the pool because he didn't know how he would handle it at all. He really wanted to get into that water, but, as he stared at it, he realized a part of him didn't even want to see how little he could do.

"So what's the problem now?" Shane asked.

Wesley turned on him. "What do you mean by *now*?"

"Swimming is now new again to you," Shane began, "so you're sitting there, staring at the water, as if it'll bite you."

"Yeah," he agreed. "It just occurred to me that, without one of my arms, I might sink."

"Before, were you a sinker or a floater?" Shane asked, with a grin.

"I was always a floater," Wesley declared.

"So do you really think that's changed?"

"I have no idea," he admitted, "but my body composition's definitely changed, and the scar tissue's changed, and everything else has to adapt, so why not that too?"

"Good point," Shane noted. "Hop in and let's see."

Wesley slowly got up on his one good leg, grabbed the railing, took a gentle hop over, and jumped into the shallow end. He knew that Shane had observed how Wesley was playing it cautious, but, wow, Shane wasn't the one with a missing leg and a missing arm. Wesley wasn't even sure how he would swim now. He could kick with one leg, but would that do anything? He could move one arm. Would that do anything? Or would he just rotate, like some spinning top in the water?

When he bounced up to the surface, the one realization that really hit him was the fact that he was actually in a pool. After all these years he was finally in a pool. Whether the outcome was good or bad, having that water surround him, over his head, on his face, it was delicious.

"Now," Shane suggested, as he crouched in front of him, "I want you to just bounce around and get used to that feeling of being in there. See what one leg feels like. See what one arm feels like."

Wesley shot him a look and declared, "You know I'm terrified, right?"

"Yep, that's why you need to figure out what your body feels like in this whole new environment. We'll spend a lot of time here, and we have a lot of muscles to work on, and we have a lot of exercises to do," he shared. "So the best thing you can do right now, and for the next few minutes, is just relax and figure out where your body's at."

"Well, my body is screaming out for the other leg," he stated. Yet, in truth, his body was relaxed. He sank down to the bottom again and realized that the one leg did just fine pushing him back up. The one arm did just fine pulling up too. When he broke through the water's surface again, he watched as Shane took notes. "It's really unnerving when you're writing notes all the time."

He grinned. "I've heard that a time or two."

"And yet you don't stop."

"How else will I get down info on what you can do and what you can't do?"

"Oh my God," Wesley muttered. "I'm in the pool for the first time, bouncing. What could you possibly write down that would be important?"

"Here's one fact," Shane pointed out, "how you're in there, willing to see what you can do and what I will tell you to do. And that's very important."

"It doesn't feel very important right now," Wesley complained, as he shifted to his back, attempting to float, using his good arm to try to hold himself up. He sank on the one side. He bounced back up, frowning.

"Your flipper is not helpless," Shane reminded him.

Wesley frowned at him, looked down at what he had remaining of his left arm, and started moving it slowly back and forth. And then he tried the same floating motion again, flopping to his back. With his one arm and the flipper both moving, he just barely stayed afloat. But—and this was the thing that was really important—he did stay up. When he got his remaining foot back under him again, Shane was grinning at him, like a fool.

"It shouldn't be that big a deal," Wesley grumbled, staring up at him and then back down at his flipper.

"Yet it feels like it, doesn't it?" Shane asked.

"Yeah, it does," he conceded. "I still have a long way to go, though."

"You sure do," Shane agreed. "Now, just cutting across the shallow end, I want you to do one length with just your legs."

Wesley frowned at him. "Yeah, you used the term *legs*. I only got one. I won't make my way across even the short side of this pool with only one leg."

Shane shrugged and declared, "A dolphin has one tail. So maybe just back that thinking up and try."

He glared at him and shook his head. "I'll just sink again."

"If you sink, then use your arms to pull yourself back up again."

At the edge of the pool Wesley braced himself and then pushed off, trying to get as far as he could propel himself, before he had to try and get that one good leg to do something. But the partial leg was already moving too, almost instinctively. Wesley was balanced awkwardly on the surface, leaning to the one side, but the one good leg—rather than kicking— was almost moving as if a dolphin tail itself. When he got to the other side, he hit it harder than he expected to. He put his leg down for balance and turned and stared up at Shane.

And once again Shane was grinning at him.

"Okay," Wesley conceded grudgingly, "some of this might be doable."

"A lot of it's doable," Shane stated. "We just have to get your mind to go there."

And that was the part that worried Wesley. He was already tired. He didn't think he could do much more today.

"Right now," Shane began, "I just want you to spend some time and float and move and just play in the water. You have no idea what it's like anymore, and now that we know that we have something there to work with," he noted, "we won't do any practical exercises today. You've already done a full workout, so just play in the water for a bit." And, with that, Shane grabbed a deck chair and sat down beside him.

"Do you have to babysit me?" Wesley asked.

"I have to babysit," he confirmed, with a nod.

"So I'm never allowed out here on my own?"

"Depends. Right now we don't have anybody out here," Shane noted, "so one of us has to be here. After we see where you're at and after you pass a certain level of tests, that's a different story." He added, "But right now? Yep, I have to be here."

It felt as if he were being babysat, an unnerving and oddly disquieting sensation. It'd been a long time since Wesley had been in a position like that. Yet he would not look a gift horse in the mouth, and he just threw himself into the water, turning, twisting, just enjoying being in the pool again. He stuck to the shallow side, so he could always put down his one good leg and touch the bottom of the pool.

And then slowly, over time, he crept down a little bit farther toward the deep end. Shane was right; Wesley needed time to just see how his body handled this. And, whenever he got into a bit of a panic, he grabbed the side of the pool and hung on for dear life. After one particularly embarrassing incident, he looked over, but Shane wasn't even looking at him. "What's the point of being on watch," Wesley asked, "if you don't watch?"

"Oh, I saw that," Shane replied. "but you still handled it yourself."

Wesley frowned at that because, of course, Shane had seen it. Wesley questioned whether he would be okay in here. He didn't want to drown while he was in the pool, which had been another disconcerting thought. Yet, so far, he'd done just fine, outside of feeling as if he were being tested by Shane. Yet wasn't that what Shane had done since day one? It was his job here. He tested Wesley to see his current capability, to see his improvements over time. Wesley sighed, remembering Shane's words about getting his mind to agree to what his body could do. With a nod, he decided to tread water in the deep end and maybe do a lap from there back to the shallow end.

Chapter 4

ALBA WALKED THROUGH the dining room, scooped up a very large cookie that was still warm and gooey, laughing as she walked over to the counter and poured herself a cup of coffee.

"What's the laughter for?" Dennis asked, behind her. She twisted to see him cleaning off tables again and refilling condiments.

"Hey, I was laughing because of the cookie."

"Most people don't laugh when they see those cookies," he replied, eyeing the cookie curiously.

"I was just teasing Dani that I would come down and get a huge cookie for myself and would not share it."

His eyebrows shot up.

"She told me flat-out that there wouldn't be any big cookies today. And that's why I was laughing, because of course there are."

"And yet you still only have one."

"I am only having one," she declared.

"Still won't take her one?" he asked.

"I am," she admitted, "but I couldn't resist chomping on mine first, but then I have to get coffee. Now I'll snag her one and share—don't worry," she added. "Otherwise she would send me back down here, as soon as she saw my cookie."

He grinned at her and nodded. "And so she should. Do you want a plate?"

"Nope, I'm fine." And, true enough, she grabbed her coffee, picked up another cookie with a napkin, and headed back down to the offices.

She stopped in at Dani's doorway and announced, "So, since you said there would be no big cookies, on that note, I decided that I wouldn't share." And she held up the remainder of her cookie that she was munching on.

Dani's eyes widened. "Why are there cookies today?" she asked, shifting over and bringing up the menu. "There are no big cookies on the menu," she cried out. She bolted to her feet, and then Alba chuckled and held out the cookie she had hidden.

With relief, Dani's face crumpled. "Do you have any idea how hard it is to get cookies and cinnamon buns around this place?"

"I figured you had a secret stash of them," she replied, "because you get more than anybody I know."

"Yeah," she muttered in an ominous tone. "And I pretty well have to bribe everybody to get them." She looked at her cookie and sighed happily. "Wow, it's huge."

"It is. It always surprises me when they make big ones like this," Alba noted, "because you would think it would serve the population better to have multiples of smaller ones that would spread around, so everybody could have at least one."

"They just make multiples of this size," Dani shared, "and most people then only take one."

"Oh, good point," Alba noted, studying the cookie. "I only took one. If they'd been smaller, I would have been tempted to take two."

"Exactly." Dani chuckled. "And there's never any such thing as leftover cookies."

"No, there isn't, is there? Especially these."

"They are some of the best, aren't they? And, of course, those are another of Ilse's family recipes."

"Right? But, hey, as long as we aren't gaining weight at this place, we should enjoy it. Though that whole weight gain thing is why I'm going out horseback riding this afternoon. What about you?"

"Love to," she replied. "I need to get Morning Star out some more."

"That's the problem with working for a living," she stated. "It impacts our hobbies."

"Hey, I'm just delighted I get to have Morning Star here where I work. I get to see her during lunch hours and evenings, afternoons, all over the place. Sometimes I just sit outside and have a cup of coffee with her."

"And so you should," Alba agreed. "I don't get out anywhere near enough with mine."

"And yet you're out there all the time too," she reminded her.

"Well, I try, but it seems, as you just mentioned, that we still don't get out there enough."

"True." Dani nodded. "When's the next therapy session on horseback?"

"We don't have any this week," Alba noted. "I think the next ones are scheduled for Tuesday." She glanced at her calendar on her e-tablet.

"Good," Dani replied. "I work a half day on Tuesday."

"You want to help out?"

"Sure, would love to. What about Wesley? Is he ready?" And then Dani stopped. "No, he isn't. That'll be a while yet."

"I think it will be a while too," Alba agreed, "but he really wants to get back to horseback riding and swimming and woodworking. Apparently he had a lot of hobbies beforehand."

"And a lot of hobbies is good because that means he will hopefully apply himself to get back to at least one or two of them. Lots of guys don't bother returning to some of their hobbies, and a lot of them can't go back to them—or at least the effort required to get back to them isn't worth it for them."

"Wesley seems to love woodworking. Apparently he made a crib for his niece."

"Oh, that's sweet," Dani said, her face softening. "That would be lovely, wouldn't it, to have an heirloom like that to hand down from family member to family member."

Dani had a point. It would be lovely to have a few heirloom pieces made by somebody who cared, not just mass-manufactured furniture, purchased because they were pretty or durable.

ALBA THOUGHT ABOUT that a lot over the next few days and mentioned it to Wesley a couple times too. She brought it up again in today's session. "I was thinking about how you mentioned making your niece a crib. Is there another woodworking project that you want to make for her that you could work toward?"

He looked at her and shrugged. "Well, she's outgrowing the crib," he replied. "So, in theory, yes."

"A princess bed," she stated instantly.

He stared at her. "Are you talking about four posters and a canopy kind of bed?" he asked cautiously.

She laughed out loud. "I always wanted one of those."

"Wow." Wesley stared off into space, thinking about it. "It might be doable. I don't know that that's what her parents want."

"Maybe not," she admitted. "But I bet if *she* had a choice …"

"That's almost like graduating to an older bed."

"Not really. You can make it a little princess bed for a little girl, and then she can choose what she wants when she reaches puberty."

He nodded thoughtfully. "It wouldn't be all that hard," he muttered. "I would want to turn the newel posts, and, of course, I would carve the headboard," he muttered out loud.

She studied him with a smile on her face. "You really do like woodworking, don't you?"

"Especially something like that for my niece," he said, with an affectionate grin. "She is a sweetheart."

"Are they planning on number two?"

"I think they are. I know they're trying." He shrugged. "Whether it happens or not, now that's a different story."

"Life's like that, isn't it?" she replied. "You can plan all you want, but life has a way of taking detours and setting you back to the beginning again."

"Isn't that the truth," he muttered, staring down at his flipper.

"And yet, with each of those challenges," she noted, "comes a chance to triumph."

He snorted, as he looked over at her. "Do you keep a card file of all these little sayings?"

She shook her head. "They come from my heart," she

murmured. "Our session's done today, but I really liked the idea of that princess bed."

"Is that part of our session?" he asked, as he slowly wheeled back to the door.

"Finding a reason to challenge yourself definitely is." She nodded. "Where are all your tools?"

"They're stored in California."

Her heart sank slightly, and then she nodded. "Where's your brother with your niece live?"

"He's here," Wesley shared. "It's one of the reasons why Hathaway House was one of my choices. I wanted to be close to family."

"And that makes as much sense as anything." She nodded. "Have they seen you here yet?"

"No, I've told them to wait, until I could get a little bit more adept."

"You mean, so that you've had a chance to adjust a little further."

He nodded. "My brother's been really good, but I hate to see pity on people's faces."

"And is your sister-in-law like that?"

He frowned, as he stared down at the floor.

"Or have you not given her a chance?"

"I haven't really given her a chance," he admitted. "I've stuck to just phone calls."

"And is that fair?" Alba murmured. "For all you know, she's very sympathetic to your plight and has a lot of experience dealing with people in difficult physical injury situations."

"Difficult physical injury situations?" he repeated, staring at her. "That's a mouthful."

"You don't like the word *handicapped*."

He winced at that. "No, I really don't. *Physically challenged* maybe. I don't know."

"How about *physically capable?*" she asked.

He smirked. "Okay, now you're really pulling on straws."

"I'll pull on whatever I have to, to keep that positive mind-set going," she admitted cheerfully.

He looked at his watch. "Four o'clock," he muttered.

"What does that mean for you?" she asked, coming out behind him. She locked the door and walked down the hallway with him.

"I'll try for the pool," he shared. "Shane told me, after I passed a few tests, that I would be allowed to go alone, but I haven't had those tests yet."

"There is usually somebody on duty or at the pool during business hours," she noted. "So you could always text him and ask him if that's close enough for his needs."

He looked at her. "Shane didn't mention that."

"He might've forgotten, and he might've thought that you weren't even close to being ready for that."

"And he might've thought that I would have gone every day."

"Have you done any PT work in the pool yet?"

"No, so far I'm getting reunited with my body in the water," he replied in dry tones.

She stared at him for a moment. "I imagine that would be challenging enough."

"Do you swim?" he asked.

"Love swimming," she said. "Haven't done a whole lot lately though."

"Come with me. You're a doctor."

"I'm not that kind of doctor," she replied, chuckling.

"Nice try."

"But you would supervise me, wouldn't you?"

"And I'm not sure that's a good idea either," she said, laughing. "I'm not a certified lifeguard. Plus you outweigh me by probably sixty pounds."

"The water helps equalize the weight differences. … You could try supervising me," Wesley added in a wheedling tone.

"Wow, there's an awful lot of a two-year-old in you surfacing right now."

He nodded. "Yep, and a four-year-old and a six-year-old, depending on what temperament I'm in," he declared, with that grin. "I'll text Shane and see if it's okay to have you supervise me. I don't want to go to all that effort of getting changed if it's not allowed. Plus it's a gorgeous day, and I would really like to decompress."

"If it's decompression for you, then absolutely," she agreed. "I can come and sit on the edge of the pool."

"Nope, if you'll come down there," he declared, "you have to swim."

"And if I don't want to?" she asked, looking at him curiously.

"What, is this another test?" he asked.

"No test," she murmured. "Just a simple question."

"Sometimes I don't think there are any simple questions here," he admitted. "It seems everybody's always looking for, waiting for, expecting some answer, and I'm always trying to give you the right answer."

"Interesting," she murmured. "I don't think that's how we feel about it at all."

"Maybe not," he muttered, "but it seems that way." He gave her a quick wave and said, "I'm taking this hallway."

And he turned, twisting to watch, as she walked down the other hallway.

IN HIS ROOM Wesley quickly got changed, while waiting for Shane to text his reply.

Roger's on lifeguard duty for another hour, so you're good to go until 5:00 p.m.

At that, Wesley rolled his wheelchair toward the elevator and down to the ground-level floor. Only when he got out, a great big Newfoundlander sprawled in his way. He looked at her, and his heart melted. "I don't know who you are, beauty," he said in a soft tone, "but you're definitely not making it easy for me to get to the pool."

At that came a call from behind him. He turned to see a man walking toward him, a genial smile on his face. "Hey, this is Helga. She lives here permanently."

Helga just reached up that big head and sniffed him. She didn't move her huge body, but, when Wesley studied her fully, he said, "Oh, wow, she's missing a leg."

"Yep, she sure is, and, if you're a sucker, then she'll milk it for all she can," the man shared, "until you're out there with the horses one day and watch her run as fast as them."

At that, Wesley burst out laughing. "Seriously?"

"Oh, yeah, she is very adept at both getting attention for her amputation and at making that amputation a nonissue." He gave a voice command and a hand command to follow it, and Helga hopped to her feet and came over to the man, her tail wagging. And, true enough, she appeared to be completely comfortable.

"How long since she lost her leg?" Wesley asked

"Quite a few years now," he replied, thinking about it. "Five, maybe."

"Interesting," Wesley murmured. "She is quite comfortable, isn't she?"

"She so is." He walked her closer and introduced them. "Helga, this is Wesley. Wesley, this is Helga."

"And how did you know I'm Wesley?" he asked, looking up at him.

He grinned right back at him. "I'm Stan. I'm the vet down here. I generally have a good idea who the new people are, and I have a note on my file to bring you a rescue animal or two to visit with, depending on who and when we both are available."

"Really?"

"Yep, and your picture's on my file," he added, with a chuckle. "So no magic involved."

"Seems like magic," he murmured.

"Ah, this place is a bit on the magical side," Stan agreed, with a bright smile. "How are you finding it, being here?"

"Well, I've been here a little more than three weeks, so I'm getting a little more comfortable with it all," he murmured. "It's still new, and it's still different, and it's still a little unnerving."

"In what way?" Stan asked.

"Because everybody expects a lot out of me," Wesley admitted, "as if this is the starting point and where I'll finally end up is a long way away from here. While I want to believe that they're correct, I also think that they're out to lunch for even expecting such progress."

At that, Stan shot him a commiserating look. "Not the first time I've heard something similar from other guys and gals. However, what I can tell you is that almost everybody here leaves in way better shape than they arrived."

"Maybe," Wesley conceded, "but will it be enough to get me back to a normal life or not?"

"I don't know," Stan stated. "How about creating a new normal. Just like Helga here."

At that came a call from the double doors in front of them. Stan pointed to them and added, "Our office and clinic are through there. Anytime you want to come see some of the animals I've got on tap, feel free. It could be a busy day, depending on how many appointments I have or if I'm doing surgeries that day," he explained, "but all the patients upstairs are welcome to come down here. Sometimes I come upstairs, looking for help," he shared. "Sometimes I've got kittens that are being nursed overnight, or maybe I've got puppies that are missing their mom and need some love," he described, "and then, of course, there's all the other therapy animals."

"Good to know," Wesley said, with a nod. "I'm heading to the pool right now. I only have until 5:00 p.m. apparently."

At that, Stan pointed him in the right direction and then walked over a few steps and hit a big button, and the double glass doors opened. "You're right there," he declared. "Enjoy." And, with that, Stan turned and walked back to his clinic.

Chapter 5

A LBA REALLY SHOULDN'T be going swimming with Wesley. Yet he was an interesting man, and anything that got him staying positive and moving in the right direction was okay by her. Besides, she didn't have any plans right now. Alba reached her onsite apartment and changed into a demure one-piece, grabbed a cover-up and a towel, a book and a pair of sunglasses, and slowly walked over to the pool area. She could see him already in the water. She stopped at the edge and smiled down at him.

When he noticed her, he turned, stood up on his good leg, and said, "There you are. I figured you chickened out on me."

"Nope, I'm here." She walked over to the closest chair, dropped her towel, book, and sunglasses, then peeled off her cover-up and walked over to the steps, and slowly made her way down. As she sank under the water and reappeared soon afterward, she noted, "It's cooler than I expected it to be."

"It's not cold at all once you get moving around," he countered. "It's really nice."

She nodded, made a clean dive under the water, and came up a good ten feet away. As her face crested through the water, she murmured, "It really is refreshing, isn't it?"

"Yes, it is. I wonder why you don't come more often."

"I tend to think of it as more for the patients," she replied, giving him a bright smile, "like you."

"Probably it is, during the day," he noted, "but what about after that?"

She nodded. "There is an *after that* every day, every evening, where the pool is available. No lifeguards or orderlies or attendants are assigned here after 5:00 p.m. though. Unless by special permission maybe. And, of course, there are often patients in the hot tub. Sometimes Shane comes down himself and has to bring somebody in for muscle cramps."

Wesley winced at that. "Honestly, muscle cramps are the worst."

"They can be, no doubt about it. You won't have to worry about it here though. They attack them as quickly as they know about them."

"I hope so. Most of those issues I've already suffered through."

"And you're doing better now?"

"Yes." He nodded. "Of course Shane has got a much harder program for me here, so maybe I'm speaking too soon."

She laughed. "It's possible," she murmured. "Sometimes we expect to be doing just fine and then find out that it's not quite so easy."

"You're right," he confirmed, "but still, I'll take what I can get right now."

"Exactly. And, if you don't mind, I'll do a few laps."

"Go for it," he said. "I'm still trying to figure out how to do that."

"I've seen people without any arms do it," she shared, looking at what remained of his left arm. "Maybe yours is more of a roll problem. I don't know, but one guy goes through the water as if he's a dolphin," she stated. "It's really amazing to watch."

AND, WITH THAT, Alba dove back under the water and started doing laps, with a clean, crisp front crawl motion that he both admired and was jealous of. He thought about what she'd said about the one guy with no arms. That would be brutal, and yet he could imagine it. He'd certainly seen videos of other people who struggled with various injuries, and yet they still managed. Maybe Wesley really was making a bigger deal out of this than it should be. And, with that thought in mind, he went under the water to just give it a try.

And was absolutely amazed that, although it took some new body movements, he was doing okay. Instead of trying to use his good right arm, he put it against his side and just rolled through the water, using his head to cleave through as he moved forward. When he came up for air, she was watching him.

"How was it?" she asked him.

"*That,*" he murmured, "was fantastic." And he pushed off and went back under again. He barely heard her laughing above the noise of the water, but it was something that he really needed to try. After he wore down, which didn't take very long at all unfortunately, he came to the pool's steps and sat down.

And there Shane stopped him and said, "You have a very interesting way to work through the water."

"But it worked though," he stated excitedly.

"It did, indeed. And, with you having one working

method," Shane pointed out, "then everything else will slowly get easier." He waved a hand in goodbye and added, "Now that you're in good hands here, enjoy your pool time." And, with that, Shane walked away.

Feeling he'd been given a pat of approval that he didn't even realize he needed, he headed back to diving in and out of the water, more like a porpoise than a human, but it felt so freeing to move the way he wanted to. By the time he was tired for the second time, he pulled out of the water and sat on the steps, realizing that Alba had gotten out of the water and was sitting poolside in a chair.

"Hey," he said, giving her a smile. "That worked out pretty well."

"Looked like it did," she agreed, returning his smile. "Honestly you looked as if you were totally in control."

"Well, I was when doing that part at least," he murmured. "There's an awful lot more to learn. Or to relearn, as it were."

"There'll always be more to learn," she murmured.

And once again he got one of those little gems of wisdom from Alba. He nodded slowly. "And sometimes," he replied, "you just need to see other people's perspectives to realize how things can work."

"Exactly." She nodded. "And I'm thrilled to see that the idea worked, although I can see that just from your legs alone, you shouldn't have any problems swimming properly. You just have to figure out how to adapt your rhythm."

"Maybe," he muttered, "but I have to tell you that I'm too tired to worry about it today."

She chuckled at that. "I am not surprised." She shifted her sunglasses onto her face and stared around her. "It's a pretty spectacular day," she murmured.

"It is. It really is." He sat here, regaining his breath. "And now the problem is, I have to get changed in order to make it up there for dinnertime."

"You and me both," she replied.

And that was just one of the really good things about her. She didn't expect him to complain about it taking him longer. She didn't expect it to be something that he would look at her and say, *Oh, well, it's easy for you. It's not so easy for me.* It was just one of those things that wasn't even an issue. She acknowledged that he would have a harder time getting changed than she would, and that was just the way it was.

What a unique view, and he still wasn't sure what to do with it. Yet he was pretty happy that it lent that level of normalcy about everything here. "I suppose I should get a start on dressing for dinner."

She nodded. "If you want, I'll meet you up there."

He looked at her. "Don't you have somebody to eat with?"

"Meaning that, if I do, I should go with them instead of with you?" she asked, a soft smile on her face.

He winced. "I'm not sure that's the way I intended it."

"And the fact that you're *not sure* that's the way you intended it is an even bigger problem," she pointed out, chuckling.

He groaned. "It seems everything's always taken the wrong way."

"It's not *always* taken the wrong way," she clarified. "Here we're very literal, so, if you need to say something, then just come out and say it."

"And that's a lesson I have yet to learn, I gather." He shrugged and stated, "I would be delighted to meet you for dinner today."

"Good," she said, as she stood up and snagged her towel. "I'll see you in what, twenty minutes?" She turned and looked at him. "Or do you want to shower first?"

He looked at his watch with the slip on elastic band and tilted his head. "A shower would be good, but I think I would rather do that at the end of the evening. And then I can go straight to bed."

"Makes sense to me. So is the twenty-minute time frame workable?"

"It is." He watched her leave and then realized that the last thing he wanted was to be late. So, if he didn't get a move on, that's what he would be.

Chapter 6

ALBA WASN'T SURE how they had fallen into it, but, following almost a sense of rhythm, they went from being friends to meeting up for a lot of their meals. It was good, but it also might complicate her ability to be detached as his counselor. She frowned as she thought about it over the next few days. And then, when Dani stopped in to ask Alba about something else, Alba brought up this issue with her boss and longtime friend.

Dani looked at her and nodded. "That's an interesting issue. Do you feel you can be detached as his counselor, even while spending more time with him at meals and such?"

"Sure. And I really like him. I like to see him challenge himself, and I like to see him get up and go farther down the pathway that he's on. He definitely has a few challenges that he can't really recognize within himself, so it's nice to spur that on," she murmured. "I just wonder if I'm creating a problem where there isn't one."

"I have no idea," Dani admitted. "However, I trust you, and so, if you feel something is there that may hinder your counseling of him, we can switch him to another doctor."

"Let's see how far along this pathway we get," Alba suggested. "It could very well be that, as he makes more friends here, he won't want to spend as much time with me. And I definitely do not want to hamper his progress. I'm so careful about that."

Dani agreed, and they left it at that.

When Dennis made a comment a few days later about her being alone for a meal, she smiled at him and replied, "I guess it is quite noticeable that we've spent a lot of time together, isn't it?"

"Of course," Dennis replied. "Hathaway is a big place, yet it's a small place. But it's not a problem."

"Maybe not," she admitted, "but I'm also his doctor."

At that, Dennis nodded slowly. "But if there's nothing between you but friends, and nothing to interfere with his rehab," he pointed out, "maybe having this level of a friendship helps you to understand who and what he really is and what he needs. Besides, spending time outside of the counseling probably goes far with these guys, being accepted in real-life situations."

"Well, it sounds good in theory," she said, with a laugh. "I'll have to think about it."

As it was, Wesley didn't join her that night, and she found herself constantly looking at her phone, wondering if there was a problem. When she didn't hear from him at all, she assumed that he had made other plans. It's not as if they had had an arrangement set, where they met every night. It just happened to be that way, as they fell into that routine. Until tonight.

When she saw him a couple days later, she was at the entrance to the dining room, waiting in line, when she heard a man beside her.

"There you are," Wesley said. "I finally caught up to you."

She looked over at him and smiled. "Hey, I just figured you got busy and made some new friends."

He shook his head. "No, I wish that was all. I just ended up feeling not so good."

She looked at him. "You were sick?"

"I'm not exactly sure that's what I would call it either," he noted, "but I ended up with a touchy tummy."

She nodded. "Oh, I'm sorry to hear that." The fact that he hadn't contacted her about it also kind of made sense because, as far as he was concerned, they were still very much a case of patient and doctor. "I didn't know about that," she shared, "because it didn't interfere with one of our sessions, or somebody would have told me about it."

He nodded. "And I wondered if I should contact you, but guess who broke his charger?"

She stared at him. "Wow, you've really had a couple of days."

"Exactly." He nodded. "But, hey, I figured you probably would have gotten the message through the grapevine."

"Nope, not at all," she said cheerfully, feeling inordinately pleased that she had a valid reason for his silence, something that didn't involve their ongoing friendship. And how foolish was that because there wasn't any reason to suspect anything other than that he had just gotten busy. "Next time, send me a message. I can bring you meals or a drink or whatever," she explained. "Just send it through the e-tablet."

He frowned at her. "I didn't even think of that," he murmured. "How foolish. I'm sorry."

She shook her head. "Gosh, no. We didn't have anything arranged, already in place, other than your scheduled appointments." And then she laughed. "In a place like this, you always have to be open to change."

He nodded, as they moved through the buffet line, keeping his voice low. "I have to admit I wasn't doing all that great these last couple days."

"And maybe there was a message sent out to your team, but, as it didn't impact my schedule, I probably didn't look at it too closely," she admitted. "I've been pretty busy."

He smiled. "I think in a place like this, we are all busy."

"And not only that, there's always the forward and backward motions, one step forward, three back," she noted. "So, it's just one of those things that we adapt to."

"Got it," he murmured. "Anyway, I'm back. I'm eating, and I'm feeling a lot better."

"Good," she said, as she studied him. "Were you not eating for a few days?"

He nodded. "Yeah, a couple of the exercises that I was doing with Shane seem to have affected my ability to digest food," he explained. "So for two days everything was just shooting right through me. We ended up switching out the program and giving everything a rest."

"Good," she replied. "People usually watch out for sore muscles, but they don't know to consider digestive issues or brain fog issues or other symptoms that it could have caused."

"Right, and I wasn't thinking that either," he admitted. "I was heading straight forward to my goals and doing really well, but my body had other ideas."

At that, she laughed. "And that's one of the main lessons here. Your body always rules. And it's up to you to listen."

"And that was one of the things that Shane pounded into me too," Wesley stated, "but I am doing better."

"And that's a good thing," Dennis said, joining in their conversation. "So, no more weak bouillon for you, *huh*?"

Wesley winced. "No, I want some real food."

"Now that was real food," he countered. "Ilse made you bone broth. Not too many people around here get that."

He nodded. "Still prefer a steak, though."

Dennis laughed. "Wouldn't we all," he muttered. "Wouldn't we all."

WESLEY SHOULD HAVE let Alba know. It only really dawned on him, after they had shared lunch, as he sat afterward in his room, thinking about how nice it was to spend time with her again and to eat a meal together. But somewhere in the back of his mind he figured that she probably had a completely different group of friends to sit with, and she was probably happy to not have Wesley around. He didn't even know how he got into that mind-set, but he was so caught up in his own world and all the pain coursing through him that his brain was on hold.

And only now, "Now," he said out loud, "as I sit in my room all alone, do I realize I was an idiot." But, hey, she didn't seem to hold it against him, so that was a good thing. As he considered that, he thought he couldn't help but think about how he was already viewing her as somebody special, as somebody he wanted to keep in touch with when this was over. But, for her, he was just one more patient. One more person who required time and energy.

Although Wesley fully believed that she would be ecstatic and excited to see his progress over his time period here at Hathaway House, there was absolutely nothing personal in it. This was all professional. And that was something he needed to keep in mind.

Chapter 7

A LBA WALKED THROUGH the next couple days, as everything appeared to be back to normal. When she saw Wesley for his next counseling session, she looked up and smiled at him, as he wheeled his way into her office. "And yet there's that painful expression on your face again," she noted.

He nodded. "Yeah, apparently I'm having some issues," he muttered.

"Do you want to reschedule?" she asked in concern.

He hesitated, shook his head, and replied, "Let's see if I can get through this."

"It's not supposed to be something to *get through*," she teased.

"Then you really have no idea how most people view sessions with somebody like you."

At that, she burst out laughing. "I do have a pretty good idea," she corrected, "and you're right. Most of the time, it's not well received, is it?"

He shook his head but managed to grin. "On the other hand, I don't mind in the least. At least this way I give you warning that I may not be there for dinner tonight."

"And you don't have to give me warning," she said gently.

He nodded. "I know, but I … It bothered me that I

didn't even make that effort."

"And I wouldn't have expected you to, not when you are so sick," she stated. "Don't ever feel guilty about stuff you don't need to. As a society we tend to rack ourselves over with guilt, and it's not something that's ever necessary here."

"Maybe not," he agreed, "but that doesn't really make me feel any better."

She chuckled. "Okay, understood."

He smiled at her. "It's … it's kinda hard because I was just more focused on me."

"And you're here to focus on you," she reminded him.

"I get that. I do." But obviously he was struggling to even maintain any semblance of lucidity.

"I'm making an executive decision," she announced, getting up and walking around her desk and coming behind him. "We're canceling today's session, and you are going to your room and going to bed. I will alert the rest of your team."

He stared at her. "Do I look that bad?"

"Yep, you sure do. Have you had a doctor check you over?"

"I was supposed to go last time, but I didn't make it," he explained. "By the time I got rescheduled, it seemed to be a nonissue."

"And yet it's now raised its head a couple times. Therefore, it's now an issue," she declared. She pulled out her e-tablet, checked on the medical doctor's schedule, and murmured, "He's in today. I'm taking you right there."

"Hey, it's not that big a deal," Wesley argued, but she wasn't listening. She pushed him down the hallway, until she got him to the medical doctor's office.

The receptionist looked up and smiled at her. "Hey.

What's up?"

"We've got a problem," she replied and quickly explained the situation. "This is the second scenario. He was supposed to come earlier and see him after the first scenario but didn't."

"In that case," the nurse stated, "let's get him right in."

Wesley protested the whole way, but neither of the women listened.

By the time he was in his own exam room, Alba told him, "Now let me know how you are afterward."

He groaned. "It's really not a big deal. You're making a fuss over nothing."

"Good," she said, "I hope it *is* over nothing. But, on the off-chance that it isn't, we'll keep making a fuss until it's settled." And, with that, she closed the door gently on him.

As she walked past the nurse with a wave, Alba took one final last look to the room Wesley was in and walked away.

WESLEY STARED UP at the doc, who was studying him with a measured look. "Yeah, I know," Wesley admitted. "I'm overdue to have this checked out."

"I'll run some tests." The doc stood, and, with the nurse joining them, he said, "Let's get some blood drawn, and we'll run him through the standard tests. Seems he's running a bit of an infection."

"I don't know where I would've got it from," Wesley pointed out, "but I am tired."

"And that's always a sign that we need to take care," the doc noted. "Your immune system's compromised, and your body is already struggling with a lot going on in its world," the doctor explained. He checked Wesley's blood pressure and his temperature, and, by the time he was done, he nodded. "We'll run the blood through our usual tests. I'm hoping it's just a simple cold."

"Me too," Wesley replied. "So why the exhaustion?"

At that question, the doctor took one step back, looked at him, and stated, "You tell me about that."

Wesley frowned. "I haven't been overdoing it—at least I don't think so."

"And how much stress are you putting on yourself?" he asked. "Do you realize what a killer stress is?"

"I hadn't really considered the stress of it all," he admitted. "I've been here a few weeks, still getting the hang of things. I figured things were calming down."

"And they probably have," the doc noted, "but they may have calmed right down into something like this because that's not unusual either."

"You mean, after a period of stress, and you're finally feeling okay, then everything blows up?" Wesley asked in amazement.

"Often it does happen that way. Your body relaxes and has a chance to deal with everything you've thrown at it, and, in its process, it's giving you a message that you need downtime."

"But I don't have very much time here," he muttered.

"You have enough time," the doctor declared firmly. "And, if we need more, then we apply for more," he added. "But right now? Your body needs rest."

Wesley groaned. "That won't make for easy sleeping."

"Are you not sleeping?" the doctor asked, eyeing him.

"Not recently, no," Wesley replied. "I have a tendency to wake up in the night and then have trouble going back to sleep."

"Do you want sleeping pills?"

"No, I don't want sleeping pills," he stated instantly. At that, the doctor frowned. "I know. I know. I need sleep."

"So, if you won't take sleeping pills, maybe you need to do some meditation or stretching exercises, something in order to unwind in the evening."

"I didn't think I was having a problem," he shared. Yet there was that level of fatigue that he half recognized on the inside. "And honestly I guess I've been tired for a long time."

"I would think so," the doctor confirmed.

"But it's a different kind of tired than not just getting sleep. It's a *tired of the whole process*. It's a *tired of having to be here*. It's a *tired of dealing with a body that's less than perfect*," Wesley explained.

"It's about making sure that you don't overwhelm yourself with stress about your future."

"Yeah, you got a magic solution for that?" Wesley asked, staring at the doc. "Like a magic solution for getting my arm back or my leg back or my career back?"

"No," the doctor replied bluntly. "And that's also why it's important that you see people here and that you do what you need to do to get your body back on target."

"It's trying. It really is."

"And, in this case, your rehab program is probably too intense," he suggested. "Even if you aren't aware of how much stress you're putting on your body, I suspect it's a classic case that you are pushing ahead too fast, even if you aren't aware of it."

"Maybe," he muttered. "But I wasn't—" And then he stopped and nodded. "So what do you suggest?"

"Bed rest."

Wesley groaned at that. "How about the pool and the hot tub?"

"Absolutely, as long as you're not following an exercise program or doing something like laps," he pointed out. "If you go, and you relax, and you just float and unwind, then that's fine. If, in the process, you move around and help your system to just calm down, that's fine too. But I don't want you doing anything that'll make your body feel as if it has to do more."

"For how long?"

"Give it a good two days, and come back to see me. We'll take it from there."

The doctor was pretty emphatic about it all. And not a whole lot Wesley could say or could do to convince the doc otherwise. As Wesley slowly made his way back to his room, he wondered whether there was anything else that he could do. Or was it literally just a matter of staying in bed for the next couple days, other than the occasional floating in the pool and a dip in the hot tub. And that limited prospect almost stressed him out more. He should have mentioned that.

As soon as he got back to his room, he sent Alba a text. **Just stressed and tired and doing too much apparently.**

She sent back a sad face emoji and a text. **A few days, just take a couple days. It could make a big difference.**

He added, **I can go in the pool and the hot tub, as long as I don't try to "do anything."** The phone rang just as he hit Send.

"And that's a really good reminder," she greeted him with. "Even though you're not aware of doing so much, in the back of your mind, you're always working out what you can do, what you can't do, going forward. And that's stress.

It's hidden stress, but it's there. It's in the background at all times," she explained. "That's what the doc's trying to get you to avoid doing."

"And how?" he asked, staring at his phone in amazement. "How? This … This life that we live, this is the hand I've been dealt. This is what I have to face. So, how am I supposed to make it any easier on myself?"

There was a smile in her tone, when she replied, "We work on it, both physically and mentally. And that's something we'll bring up in the next session."

"Which, if I listen to him, can't be for a few days."

"Good," she said. "It's scheduled for next week because today was obviously a wash. Maybe I'll bring that forward." She seemed distracted, as she checked out her schedule.

He brought up his e-tablet too and muttered, "I don't want to leave it too long."

"No, and physical exhaustion is one thing, but mental stress is a completely different thing," she shared. "We do have to nip that in the bud, before it gets any more prevalent."

"Yeah, good luck with that," he muttered, hating that there was just so much bitterness in his words.

Her tone softened. "I know it's hard to step back, but you are doing wonderfully well."

"It feels as if I *was* doing wonderfully well, and now I've suffered a major setback."

"The setback would happen no matter what," she stated. "All you were doing was hiding the fact that you had adjusted well, but now the deeper issues, the bigger issues, are surfacing, as you finally get some of the other issues off your plate. These have the freedom to come up, and now we must deal with them."

"Yeah, but to spend a couple days on bed rest?" he asked, with a wealth of disgust in his tone.

She laughed. "Well, if that's the case, I'll bring dinner to you tonight."

"Oh my God," he said, "that means I have to eat in bed too. That was rough when I was sick here a few days ago."

"Sure, and, if you don't listen to the doctor, that's where you'll spend an awful lot of the next couple months," she pointed out calmly. "So be thankful for a two-day reset than a two-month reset. Also, at 5:00 p.m., watch for me, as I come around with plates."

"Well, make it lots," he grumbled, "because, if I have to sit here and do nothing, I'll want to eat."

"And maybe you need to eat," she noted. "And maybe we need to get you some of Dennis's special green drinks."

"I don't like the sound of that," he replied in horror. "That sounds like, you know, kale kind of stuff."

At that, she burst out laughing. "And you could be right," she agreed cheerfully. "Dennis does have quite the shakes, nutrient shakes. I'll go talk to him now."

"Oh, *great*," Wesley muttered. "And here I was hoping for a steak."

"Maybe you'll get the steak too." And then she stopped and clarified, "Maybe you get the steak, *as long as* you have your shake."

"That sounds like blackmail," he protested.

"Yep," she agreed, "whatever works." And, with that, she hung up.

He stared down at the phone, but a smile was on his face. He settled back in his bed, hating the fact that he was even here. It's not where he thought he should be at this point in his life, and yet it really didn't seem to matter what he thought because this is what had been presented. Wesley looked up to see Shane, leaning against the doorway, his arms crossed over his chest. "I know. I know, I know. Apparently I've had a setback," he admitted, raising his one hand in frustration.

"Remember how I tell you to speak up when the exercises get past a certain tolerance point?"

Wesley frowned, his gaze cutting away.

"I get it," Shane began. "You want results. You want 'em fast. You have this deadline in your head, based on funding, or just getting out of here and on with your life. I totally understand. But remember that Dani is a whiz at getting more funding, at getting you more time. So give that thought a rest. This is your body sending you a message. Listen to your body," Shane stated, "but I don't want to lose all our gains."

Wesley looked at him hopefully. "So you'll get me a pass to work out?"

"Nope," he replied, "but you will do a whole lot of stretches from bed."

"Really?" he asked, frowning at him in disgust.

At that, Shane laughed. "That's exactly what I meant, stretches. And, if we can get you into some of those yoga poses, even better."

He stared at him in horror. "No, no, no, no, no, no. You don't understand. Yoga's not, … *not* part of this equation."

"Yeah, how come?" Shane asked, keeping his face straight.

Wesley glared at him. "I don't do yoga."

"Whether you do yoga or not," Shane replied, "these stretches are non negotiable. We might as well just get started right now."

"How is that bed rest?" he asked, immediately trying to backtrack.

At that, Shane laughed. "Bed rest is one thing. Stretches are a completely different thing. Believe me that the doc will be all over this."

"Maybe we should check with him to be sure," Wesley suggested craftily.

Shane studied him, with one eyebrow raised. "Really? Are you trying to avoid stretches? You can do a full-on rehab workout, but you can't be bothered to do a few stretches, *huh*? Or you'll cry like a baby?"

"I'm not a baby," he countered instantly. "And stretches are one thing, but I've already been threatened with Dennis's green drinks," he muttered in disgust. "Now you're talking yoga."

As if on cue, Dennis appeared around the doorframe. "What did I hear about my wonderful green drinks?" he teased, holding up a large tall glass. "This is chock-full of nutrients, greens, vitamins, and even a mineral supplement," he declared, with a mock frown on his face. "I'll have you know that these are highly prized."

"Sure, if you're a horse," Wesley complained, staring at the vivid bright-green drink coming toward him. The two other men smiled.

"You'll get through it," Shane noted. "Remember that, if you want to recover, if you want to get on and to have a full life, you must build up your strength, so that setbacks like this don't continuously happen."

"It's hardly continuous," Wesley protested.

"Twice in two weeks is continuous in my book," Shane declared. "I'm trying to stave off a third one."

At that proclamation, not a whole lot Wesley could do

but take his medicine.

Dennis held out the drink, and Wesley slowly accepted it. "Does it taste as horrible as it looks?" he asked, grimacing.

"Doesn't matter if it does. All of it down, right to the last drop. And you'll get at least one a day, maybe two," Dennis promised. "Then, when it's gone, *all* gone, you can have dinner."

He groaned at that. "Again with the blackmail," he muttered.

"Yep, whatever it takes." And, with that, Dennis was gone.

Shane looked over at him, a smile on his face, and shared, "They're actually quite good."

"Sure, if you're into grape nuts and granola and a lot of green vegetables," Wesley grumbled. "Personally I prefer my sausage and eggs and hash browns."

"Yeah, I get it, but that won't be the answer right now." And, with that, Shane motioned at the drink and said, "Go. Bottoms up." And, with that, he disappeared too.

At least they left him on his own, yet *oh my God*. Wesley looked at the drink, plugged his nose, and started to drink.

Chapter 8

OTHER THAN VISITING at mealtimes, when her schedule allowed, Alba watched over Wesley closely for the next few days but from a distance. She caught several times where he'd been handed a bright green drink and saw the look of chagrin on his face as he was forced to drink it. Not that anybody stood over him, but they were waiting. And that obviously alone was something Wesley did not like. Neither did he like the green drink.

She walked up to him three days later and smiled. "You're looking so much better. Must be all those green drinks," she teased.

He shot her a look. "Those things are nasty," he murmured.

"They aren't that bad," she argued, with a headshake. "Whenever there's a spare, I get one myself."

He stared at her in shock. "You mean, you *willingly* have one of those?"

She smiled and laughed. "Absolutely."

"You're nuts. Those things are nasty."

"I wonder if they put more things in yours than they do in ours," she murmured. "The fact of the matter is, you're depleted, and your system needs more nourishment."

"Which is why I have to drink those nasty green concoctions all the time," he muttered. "But, so far, nobody's convinced me that they're good for me because I'm not seeing any results, and they really do taste awful." He thought about it for a moment. "I suppose they probably are adding extra to mine."

"If that makes you feel better, it's all good," she noted cheerfully. She pointed toward the dining room. "Are you heading in there?"

"No, I was heading down to you."

"I was going to grab a coffee before our session," she said, checking her watch. "You're a little early."

"I know, but, timing-wise, I didn't want to just sit in my room."

"Makes sense," she said. "So come on. Let's go get a coffee, and we can take it back to my office."

He nodded, and they fell in together, heading down the hallway. At the dining room she poured coffee for two and looked over to see him with his hand dancing between two large cookies.

"I'll take the one you don't want," she offered.

He looked up, gave her a fat smile, and declared, "I was planning on both of them."

She burst out laughing. "In that case, have at it."

She walked over and scooped up one, an oatmeal cookie, and said, "I'll meet you back at the office."

She walked away deliberately. She didn't want to wait. She didn't want to help him per se. She just wanted to see how he would handle it. He came up behind her, and, as he coasted up close, she realized he really did have two cookies between his last two fingers.

She shook her head, a chuckle escaping. "What is there about cookies and men?"

"What is there about cookies and *everyone*," he clarified.

"Let's not get sexist over this. Cookies are cookies. They should be a main food group." He took a big bite, even as he coasted toward her office. Then, with a happy sigh, he added, "These really are good cookies."

"I think all the food here is good."

"Agreed, and it's really hard when people ask, *Hey, what's your favorite dish?* I just … I can't narrow it down to just one thing," he stated, with a headshake. "It's all just so good."

"And that should be a good thing overall," she added, looking at him.

"It is, but some things are just that much better than *good.*"

"Meaning that anything that counts as a cookie is that much better?" she quipped.

"Well, I hadn't thought that I was quite so particular about my sweets," he conceded, "but I must admit that cookies do take the cake."

She had a good laugh about that. Now at her office, she quickly led the way inside. "Grab your seat."

"Meaning, just roll up and park," he murmured.

"How's the leg doing?"

"The leg's not bad," he shared. "The sore on the underside's healed up."

"Still tender from too much pressure? I understand that you're getting the modified prosthetic for your leg adjusted."

"They're coming to do a fitting soon," he stated, with a nod. "Shane wants to be there to confirm that the pressure points will be where he wants them."

"Oh, good," she said. "In that case I have no doubt you'll be in good hands."

"It seems as if Shane's into so many different things,"

Wesley noted. "He's a little bit everywhere."

"And that's because the work he does is a little bit everywhere. He started off as straight physio, but he's done so much extra training that he's pretty well involved in all aspects of recovery now."

"Except yours."

"Except mine," she agreed, "but, having said that, mine is very much integrated with everything that they see too."

"I get that," Wesley noted. Then he picked up the second cookie and let out a contented sigh. "Really glad I got a second one."

"At the moment I'm kinda jealous," she admitted, laughing. "You're enjoying it so much that you make me want a second one."

He offered, "I'll share it with you."

She shook her head. "No, I'm good. I don't really have any reason to eat a second one."

"Luckily I don't need a reason," he stated, and he chomped down with a decided *crunch*.

"What kind is that one?" she asked curiously.

"A gingersnap."

She raised an eyebrow. "I didn't see those there."

"That's why I was having so much trouble deciding what to get," he explained. "It was there, and I couldn't resist." He was busy eating away again.

She asked him, "Now that we've dealt with the leg, how's the arm?"

He looked down at it and flapped it in the air. "It's here," he noted, "though it's not exactly much stronger."

"The new program that Shane's given you, is that helping?"

He shrugged. "Maybe."

"And maybe not?"

"And maybe not," he agreed, with a nod. "It's kinda hard. I want it to do so much more, but I'm limited."

"Of course you are, yet a lot of that limitation is in your head."

He winced at that. "I get that. Yet you have to also understand that this limitation is also very physical."

"Absolutely," she declared. "So what will you do about it?"

"I'll talk to the prosthetic guys, when they come for the fitting on my leg, and see what options I have for the arm."

"Oh, that sounds good," she replied, feeling happier about that. At least he wasn't walking away from it, but he was at least looking at what he had for possibilities. "You had an arm prosthetic before, correct?"

"Yes, but it was almost more work than it was worth."

"How are the nerve endings on that stump?"

"I did have extra surgery to build up a good pad there," he shared. "And the last arm prosthetic was temporary, so I'm hoping that there will be something that will improve on that one."

"And yet they're only coming to look at your leg?" she asked curiously.

"Yeah, one thing at a time. Shane says the arm is not really strong enough yet to support a prosthetic."

"Well then, you should listen to Shane."

"It doesn't mean that I can't see what my options are though," he murmured. "That might keep me a little more positive than anything."

"It can," she noted, "as long as you realize that you're in a state of flux, constantly improving and getting stronger, so keep that in mind."

"You mean, if I don't get an answer that I like when they visit?"

"Yep, absolutely. If they say they can do nothing more, how will you feel?"

"I'll feel shocked," he admitted. "That's not what I want to hear."

"Of course not, and it doesn't mean that that will be what you hear. It just means that it's not what you *want* to hear."

At that, he nodded. "It still would suck though."

"But it doesn't have to be the be-all and end-all."

HOWEVER, IT WOULD be, but Wesley didn't dare say that. "Maybe not." And he stared off into the distance. "I imagine, if I don't get a good prognosis, then I will probably end up back here in tears." He was so blunt and matter of fact about it that he couldn't consider anything else.

"In that case, do you want to book an appointment for afterward?" she suggested.

"No, I'm still hoping that I get good news."

"And if you don't? I think you need to accept the fact that you might need a second opinion."

He looked at her in surprise and then beamed. "For a moment there I was afraid you would say that I might need to accept the limitations of what I have."

"I wouldn't say that," she declared. "I think you just have to accept that it'll be a journey."

"Definitely a journey," he agreed. "And some journeys are okay. Others just plain suck."

She grinned. "You don't exactly get to refund your ticket

on this journey," she murmured. "So, how about we go through some of the things that you can do with your arm as it is, and then some of the things that a prosthetic would help you with."

"Depending on what's available on the market for prosthetics," he began, "I could get full functionality back."

"Are you in dreamland right now?" she asked.

"I would hope not, but I guess it's possible," he conceded.

"Have you done any research on it?"

He nodded. "That woman in New Mexico does some pretty spectacular things."

"And that won't be covered by insurance, I suppose."

"No, of course not," he replied, raising his good hand. "What'll be covered will be a generic one, just like what I had, with maybe a slight improvement."

"And what about funds?" she asked. "Have you contacted this woman to get a ballpark estimate? A time line estimate on making one?"

"I can contact her," he replied. "Doesn't mean she can help me or isn't booked up for two years or something."

"Maybe you should send her your medical records and see."

He stared at her, his gaze lighting up. "Maybe I will."

"All she can do is give you an idea of what might be possible, and I think, at the moment, that's what you're really looking for, to know what could be the best outcome, and then maybe an idea of what reality will look like. It could be that best outcome, but it could also be something completely different but better in some way."

"But the thing is," he admitted, "as long as I don't make those calls, there's hope."

"*Ah*," she murmured, with a long-drawn-out sigh. "Very true. As long as you have hope, you have everything, don't you?"

He nodded. "And I don't want to lose that."

"And yet you're afraid to move forward because you're afraid to lose that."

"It's not that I'm afraid to move forward because I'll lose hope," he clarified. "I just feel as if maybe I'm not ready."

"Not ready to hear the truth?"

"I didn't say that," he protested.

"But you did, though," she replied, studying him intently. "The question is, whether finding out the truth will be something you believe."

"Of course I'll believe it."

"What about a second opinion?"

"Oh, … right."

"I guess that's what you're saying, isn't it? That, even if this woman, who apparently does so much of this specialty work, if she can't help you, maybe that's not the end result."

"Right," he acknowledged, his fingers strumming away on the arm of his wheelchair. "Still, it's scary."

"It's all scary," she agreed, with a head tilt. "That doesn't mean it's not worth doing."

"Sure, but again, if it's back to that bad news thing, I'm not sure I want it."

"Maybe you aren't ready, but maybe it'll help you to decide to do better with what you've got."

"No." He shook his head. "I don't think it will. I think it'll make me angry."

"Angry because of your circumstances?"

"Sure. It'll just make me angry that I can't have what I want." And, with that, he announced, "I'm done for today." And he turned and wheeled out of the room.

Chapter 9

"THAT WENT WELL," Alba muttered for probably the umpteenth time that day. As she walked into the dining room for dinner that night, she looked around but saw no sign of him.

As she stepped up to Dennis, he asked, "Trouble?"

She shrugged. "Only when we don't like the truth."

"And yet you still deliver it anyway."

"It's my job," she murmured quietly, so nobody else could hear.

"Sometimes your job sucks though, doesn't it?"

She looked over at him, hearing the compassion in his tone. "Where is he?"

"He's having dinner over on the side with the other guys."

"Good. He needs some adjustment time."

"Seems you do, too."

She smiled at him, but there was that tinge of sadness. "You know when you like somebody but you can't allow that to stop you from doing what needs to be done?"

"Yep, I hear you," Dennis said. "And I appreciate that you're doing what you need to do that is the best for him, even if it hurts you and him."

"But he doesn't appreciate it," she whispered, "yet I get that. I have to be honest, sometimes I'm harsh maybe, in order to deal with the truth."

"And it's your job, which has always kept you apart from the others here, hasn't it?" he asked curiously, as he slowly served up her food.

She nodded. "It's one thing to watch all the relationships here, but you see that they don't have to deal with some of the harder issues," she murmured. "Or at least when you do, some of those issues come across, maybe better than the ones that I had to deliver."

"Right." Dennis handed her a plate. "Go and enjoy. Your body needs food, even when your soul's suffering."

"My soul will be just fine," she replied. "It's not the first time I've had to be a bit of a bad-news bearer."

He shook his head. "You come from the heart, and, even though they might not appreciate it right now, they will later."

She nodded, but she couldn't see the appreciation yet. She headed out to the deck, walking past Wesley, as if she didn't see him. Which, in truth, she didn't. If Dennis had not mentioned where Wesley was, she wouldn't have known. And neither did Wesley call out to her. Which said a lot. She sat here by herself at the table for a long time, eating slowly.

Dennis came out to visit for a while. He took a look at her plate and pointed. "You need more food than that."

"Yeah, but, if I eat on an upset stomach, I'll suffer later."

He nodded. "Got it. Do you want a fancy coffee?"

She looked at him in surprise. "What does that mean?"

"How about a latte?" he murmured.

"I would love one," she said. "Then I think I'll go into town."

"Sounds good. What will you do?"

"Maybe a little bit of shopping, hit the bookstore," she

muttered. "I'm off for the next two days, so I could use the break."

"In that case, the coffee won't hurt either." He disappeared and returned a few minutes later with a big foamy concoction in an Irish-motif coffee cup. He sat down beside her.

"I never even see you eat," she shared. "Why don't you join me?"

"I'll eat with the kitchen staff later," he replied. "One of the guys is having a tough time."

"*Right*." She nodded. "Even when we're not on duty, we're on duty."

"I don't think it's so much that we're on duty. I think it's just a case of we're here, and people need support, so we give it. We don't really count the cost to our time because it's who we are," he shared. "Any more than counting the cost of the bad news is something that you would hold against them."

"No, of course not," she agreed. "But it does get to be a bit much at times."

"Time for a change?"

"No," she declared, "just enough of the good things are happening around here that I wouldn't want to do that."

"Hold that thought," Dennis said, with a smile. "Because we do have a lot of good things happening, so it does keep you a little better focused."

"Oh, I'm focused," she muttered sadly, "but that focus comes with a price tag."

He nodded. "And it's one that you're willing to pay."

"I've paid it this time," she stated, as she sipped her coffee. "I wonder how many more times before I decide that relationships just aren't worth it?"

"I think, when love happens, it happens, and you don't really get a choice," he murmured. "It's not as if you set out to get to know him or that you set out to realize just what a special person he is."

"No, I didn't," she admitted. "I just fell into it."

"I think that's partly what this is all about. If you could have protected your heart, you would have, but sometimes our hearts aren't what needs protecting."

"Oh, I agree," she declared, "but I've seen so many happy relationships around this place that I just wondered if maybe …"

"Of course you did," he said, smiling. "And yet, when you think about it, happy relationships aren't something that happen overnight. We've seen every one of them hit the rocks, before people pick up and realize what's important."

She stared down at her coffee cup. "And when they don't realize it?"

"Then it wasn't meant to be," he replied. "And that's absolutely a bad-news answer for you right now."

"We aren't even that far along," she muttered, "but it's kinda like pulling the wings off a butterfly. They're already hurting here, and sometimes I have to deliver life in a hard-knock package."

"And again they don't appreciate it—yet. However, it is definitely something that's worthwhile doing."

She flashed him a grin. "I get it. Not to worry. I won't quit or anything like that. It's definitely not that bad."

"Good, but, just like everybody else here, we hate to see you suffer."

"I'm not suffering," she murmured. "Sometimes other people suffer, and you can't do anything to help."

"But sometimes they need to have a pity party and to

suffer for a bit, before they straighten up and shake off that mood. Then sometimes it's not even that, but they don't know how to get out of the doldrums."

"And sometimes they're so stuck in suffering that they don't even know what they're doing."

"That's called wallowing," Dennis noted.

She burst out laughing. "Oh, I won't argue with you there. Though, when you start to wallow, it gets to be a habit."

"And I can't argue with that either," Dennis replied. "So head off to town, have a good evening and a couple days off. We'll see how you feel when you come back."

"It's not so much how I feel," she muttered. "It's whether there'll be any progress on his side."

"Oh, there'll be progress," Dennis declared. "However, you can't guarantee in what direction it'll travel." And, with that, Dennis stood. "I have to go back to work."

WESLEY REALIZED IT had been a childish thing to do. They'd met for dinner for weeks, and now, last night, after their session, Wesley had been persuaded to go sit with a bunch of other guys. In fact, he'd initiated it, needing a distance from her more than anything. But when he'd seen her arrive, he hadn't been friendly. She'd walked right past him and sat all alone out on the deck. And, for the first time, at that moment, he realized how solitary her life must be.

As one of the therapists here at Hathaway House, she had to deliver a lot of hard truths. And yet it wasn't so much that she *had* to deliver them as she *had* to point out that he was ignoring a few. He'd already decided to speak with her the next day, but, when he went to her office that morning, it was locked up. He frowned at that and tried later. And again locked. He waited for another day and still the same. Finally he asked Shane, "Where's Alba been lately?"

"She's on her days off," he replied absentmindedly, as he studied the laptop and some of the video he'd just taken. "Okay, let's take a look at that arm of yours. I want you to do these stress tests again."

Wesley stared at him. "I just did them." He pointed to the video on pause on Shane's screen.

"Yep, and we'll up the voltage now."

And, with that, they upped the weight and did a couple of the exercises. By the time he was done, Wesley was sweating profusely. "So," Wesley muttered, gasping for breath.

"Yep, I hear you," Shane noted, "but honestly the arm is coming along nicely."

"Says you."

Shane shook his head. "Nope, says the video. Remember the testing we did when you first got here?" he asked. "Even a napkin, a piece of paper, was hard for you to keep in place under your little wing. Now look at this."

Wesley watched Shane's video from today, as Wesley slowly raised and lowered five-pound weights hung onto his partial arm. "It's definitely getting stronger then, but it's still only one-quarter of an arm."

"It is. But I also see some nerve endings coming awake," Shane declared. "So that's also very much some significant progress."

"Play that again?" Wesley asked. And he watched as his arm continued to shift and move. "It definitely looks better," he admitted. "Not that I'm quite ready to say it's *there* yet."

"No, it's not there at all," Shane confirmed, "but it's progress. When are the guys coming to look at your leg prosthetic?" he asked.

"Tomorrow. And we'll see about what, if any, improvements they could make with the arm prosthetic too."

Shane nodded at that. "It'll be interesting to see what they say."

"Have you had very many guys through here with missing arms?"

"Lots," Shane said. "Yet every situation is unique. It depends on whatever muscle they have—muscle, movement, bone, skin—whatever the stumps have left. In some cases, more surgery's required."

"I already had more surgery to build up my arm stump," Wesley said.

"So then you should be good to go."

"Maybe, but what I had for a prosthetic last time wasn't very helpful, whether for the arm or the leg."

"But each was also a prototype, wasn't it? Just beginner ones?"

"Sure, but it seems as if the arm one didn't do very much."

"But your arm was weaker back then, and your leg wasn't fitted properly, leaving a lesion as well. Still, let's see what they have to say about prosthetics when they get here tomorrow," Shane said. "Fact of the matter is, there's still an awful lot of room for this technology to grow and to improve. It'll take somebody who's on the cutting edge to know what you're capable of doing and what technology is capable of assisting you."

"*Right*," Wesley agreed, his thoughts going back to the woman in New Mexico. "Have you heard of this Kat somebody in New Mexico?"

"Yep, sure have. She does amazing work."

"She'll also be expensive, *huh*?"

"I imagine," he guessed. He turned to look at him and asked, "Did you contact her?"

"Not yet. Dr. Fendrick suggested it though."

"I would wait until tomorrow and see what the prosthetics guy says, and then I would definitely contact her. She's doing some pretty unique stuff."

"But does it work?"

"It has to work for you, and she can probably point you in the direction of somebody who's got some of her work, so you can talk to them. I would suggest you get those recommendations before you go down that pathway and get an idea on costs and how far out she's booked too."

"Right," he noted. "I didn't think about talking to somebody who has one of her pieces."

"How else will you know whether Kat's pieces work or not?" he asked. "The fact of the matter is, even if you do talk to somebody, it doesn't guarantee that they'll have the information you want because their scenario will, again, be completely different."

Wesley took those words back to his room later that afternoon, and he looked up the website for this woman. Studying it, he realized that she had all kinds of prosthetics on her site. However, she also made it very clear that there was absolutely no one case where *one size fits all*. He composed an email and sent it off, before he gave himself a chance to question it.

At least with an email, all he had to do was send in his inquiry. It wouldn't guarantee an answer, but, if it gave him something to go on, that would help. At least he hoped.

When he looked at some of the sample pictures on her website, he saw no reason why some of these wouldn't work for him. And he had already been through the surgery to prep both his stumps. So, it would all be about the cost, about what was doable for him.

Yet, for the first time in a long time, after seeing those images, he felt more positive about everything going on in his life. Except for Dr. Fendrick. He should never have walked away from Alba like he had. Talk about acting like a two-year-old. And instead of being an adult about everything, he'd blamed the messenger.

Still, all she'd done was her job. And that just reminded Wesley that most of their relationship was based on her being his counselor.

Chapter 10

WALKING INTO WORK the next morning, Alba unlocked her office door and then headed to the dining room for coffee.

Dennis looked up from setting out an assortment of clean utensils for everyone, and he smiled immediately. "You look much better."

"Yeah, a couple days off helped a lot," she admitted. "I picked up a couple books, and I've just been lazing around, enjoying life."

"Good. I approve."

She chuckled. "How about you?"

"Hey, it's all been good," he replied.

"Yeah, when was the last time you took a day off?"

"I take them off," he said, with a shrug, "but not very often. I would rather take half days all the time instead of being here every day."

"Oh, I hear you. I still think it's a good break, though, to get away from here. I'm feeling much better."

"And that's huge. Do you want a cinnamon bun to go with that coffee?"

She looked at him and smiled. "Okay, if you'll twist my arm, fine. I'll let it be twisted."

He chuckled. "Might tell Dani that they just came out of the oven."

"Don't even bother," she replied. "Give me a plate for her too."

With that, Dennis went into the back and brought out two plates with a warm cinnamon bun on each. Carrying them awkwardly and the coffee cups, she headed back in the direction of the offices. As she came around the corner, she saw Wesley talking to Shane. She carried on without saying anything, and, as soon as she made it to Dani's office, she kicked her door gently with her foot.

Dani opened the door, took one look and grinned. "I had a meeting this morning, and I was worried I wouldn't get one."

"Well, here's yours," Alba said, with a smile.

"How were your days off?" Dani asked.

"Excellent," she said.

"You look better."

"I am better. I feel a lot more balanced, so it's all good." And, with her cup and plate, she returned to her office.

As she sat down, Shane poked his head in. "Hey."

"Hey," she said, with a smile. "What's up?"

"Wesley has his fitting for his prosthetics today."

"Good. Let's hope there's some grace in that for him today."

"Exactly. Did you want to be there?"

She shook her head. "Nope, I sure don't, and I'm fully booked."

"Okay. ... Just so you know, I think he wanted you there."

She frowned at him. "I don't think so," she countered cautiously.

"But I do," he said. "I'll see how it goes. Don't be at all surprised though if you get an unexpected phone call, asking you to come down."

"Why would that happen?" she asked, studying him carefully.

"He's tried to find you several times over the weekend."

"Interesting," she murmured, staring off into the distance.

"Why? Is there a problem between you two?"

She shook her head. "No, not necessarily. I just had to do my job and mentioned a few things that needed to be said."

Shane looked at her with that way-too-perceptive gaze and smiled. "I don't know if it was a good thing or not, but he's not holding anything against you."

"That's good," she said. "It'll make it easier for our work together as we go forward."

"Are you trying to put him back into a work slot?"

She winced. "Is that what it looks like?"

"Yeah," Shane admitted. "And I can see why you would want to do that to a certain extent. However, I'm not sure it'll work in this case though."

"Why not?"

"Because, as a general rule, I would say his progress, and a lot of that progress, is because of you."

"Not so sure about that," she argued, with a gentle smile. "It's not always the best position to be in when I have to sometimes be the bad guy."

"And here I thought you were always trying to get them to be the bad guy themselves."

"Sometimes, when they don't get it," she admitted, "I do have to nudge them in the right direction."

He smiled at that. "Whatever nudging you did hasn't been a negative. I can see that maybe you guys still have some things to work out, but today's likely to be an emotional day for him."

She frowned at that. "That's true," she muttered. "If you need me, call me."

"Will do." And, with that, Shane disappeared down the hallway.

WESLEY WAITED ANXIOUSLY for his prosthetics appointment in a completely different area of the center than he had been in before. When he finally rolled his way in, he was surprised to see a couple guys already here. They had an assortment of prosthetics—legs, parts, pieces—and a big tool kit. Wesley rolled up and greeted them. "Hey. I think it's my appointment next."

One of the men looked up and smiled. "Wesley, by any chance?"

"Yeah, that's me," he said, with relief. "I can't tell you how much I've been waiting for this leg."

"We've made some adjustments to it," the other man added, speaking from behind the laptop. He poked his head out and greeted him too. "Hey, Wesley."

"Oh, Stephen, I'm glad to see you," Wesley said. "Any luck with that back section?"

"Yeah, we've taken out the hard material and put a completely soft backing on it, so there won't be anything hard pressing against that part of your leg. How is it healing?"

"It's much better," Wesley shared.

And, with that, the next hour was all about taking new measurements, testing the muscle, testing the nerves. As Wesley waited with bated breath, the prosthetic leg came out, ready for use. Then baby powder was put all over his partial leg, and a new stocking went over his stump and then onto the leg portion. The stocking was a weird netting material, different from the one he'd had before. Then the new prosthetic went over his stump and up part of his leg portion. Once secured, Wesley raised and lowered his leg to get a feel for his new prosthetic and smiled. "It feels pretty good. It's sticky, isn't it?"

The men laughed.

Stephen added, "Hey, once we get your prototype done, you can get as fancy as you want. Now, the moment you've been waiting for," he said, and he reached out a hand.

Wesley accepted the help onto his new leg and stood, not putting his full weight on it.

"You still have to put your weight on it," Stephen pointed out, eyeing him carefully. "We won't know how it works otherwise."

"It feels high," Wesley said. "Did you guys adjust it?"

Immediately one of the men, the first guy, dropped into a crouching position in front of Wesley and made an adjustment. "How's that?"

Wesley nodded. "I think that's better." And he slowly, with his full weight on it, stood free of help. His grin was a mile wide. "God, I remember how this felt before. Nothing like being back on your legs." His spirits rose the higher and the stronger he stood. "Oh, thank God," he muttered.

"You know it doesn't matter to everybody," Stephen said, looking at him.

"It matters to me," Wesley stated. "I understand that I'll always be missing the leg, but it doesn't … It won't *show* the same."

"And appearances bother you the most?" Stephen asked.

"No, but I would like to get rid of the wheelchair," Wesley admitted. "It's definitely cumbersome and a hindrance."

"And yet nice to have," Shane added from the doorway, "for when you're tired."

He looked over at him, grinned, and agreed. "Absolutely. But you can bet I'll work at not being tired enough that I have to go back into it again."

"Understood," Shane replied. "How does the new leg feel? You'll have to take a few steps and test it."

He took a tentative step, his arms out in case he fell. "It feels good," he murmured. "I don't know why I'm even acting like it's, … as if I'll fall over," he admitted. "I had this prosthetic leg, or something like it, before, and without any problems walking, except for the lesion. But it feels …" He hesitated to say it. "I don't know. It feels different."

Shane nodded. "Your muscles are different now. They're much more developed. But you should feel more stable, not more insecure."

"I don't think I'm feeling more insecure." He hesitated, trying to explain what he was really feeling. "I guess it's just the *different* part that makes it hard for me to explain it to you," he murmured. "But last time I do remember that it was hard to get used to it. It always felt as if I would fall over. I didn't trust it. But this doesn't feel the same."

"And maybe that's more so because you can trust yourself now a little more. If you do start to lean over or start to fall, you know that your other leg is strong enough to jump into action and to help rescue you."

"Maybe." He frowned at Shane. "How does it look?"

"It looks high," he suggested. He walked around to the front and squatted, eyeballing it. "I think it needs to come down a little bit more." He looked at Stephen. "I'm thinking an eighth of an inch."

Stephen stepped back, took a look at his leg, and nodded. "Let's get some measurements going on the knee and the other side," he suggested to his helper. "And we'll line them up."

It took a little longer than Wesley had expected, but then he was back up again on his new leg and walking ever-so-slowly. Just able to get vertical again and to know that this would be with him and that there were no problems with it and that he could keep it for now, all made him feel so much better. He sighed happily. "You guys have no idea how much I appreciate this."

"It's what we do," Stephen stated, with a bright smile. "Now, what about that arm?"

"I was going to ask you about that. Are we done with the leg?"

"We're done for the moment, until you tell me if anything sores up, if anything like that is going on," Stephen explained. "So I want you to walk around while we talk and get comfortable with the new leg and let me know what you're feeling, how it feels. Is it freely moving? Is it stable? And then we'll take it off, and we'll take a look at any sore spots."

And that's what they did. While they walked around and gave him time to process the weight and the feel of the new leg, he asked them what was available for his arm.

"Nothing's really changed," Stephen admitted. "Until you develop more muscle in that arm, we can't hang very much off of it that's usable."

"So a chest strap and something popped over the top is what you guys have in mind temporarily?" Shane asked.

"Yep, but, if you can get those arm muscles back and the

nerve tendons firing, that would help a lot. We haven't even gotten close to testing that," Stephen noted. "You did have corrective surgery on that stump, didn't you?" he asked, looking at him suddenly. Wesley nodded. "Then we can take a look at the nerves and see what's an option. If we've got something, we might do surgery and put in something a little more permanent. At least something that can trigger fingers opening and closing, arms raising and lowering, things like that," Stephen detailed. "So there is potentially quite a bit that we can do."

"That would be good," Wesley said, feeling such a huge sense of relief.

"Feels as if maybe there's hope after all?" Shane asked Wesley, with a knowing smile.

"It really does. I know it's stupid, and I'm grateful to be alive and to have all my faculties right now," he acknowledged, "but I need two working arms."

"And a working leg apparently," Stephen added, with a smile.

"Definitely," he murmured. "And, laugh all you want, but nothing quite like looking and acting like the rest of the world around you. Being *normal* is when you're healthy and happy and confident in your physical body," Wesley declared, "and is something that people joke about all the time. However, being *normal* when you're not normal, when the world looks at you differently and sees where you are different and how you look different," Wesley added in an impassioned speech, "it can become something that you crave."

"You'll feel—and look—a whole lot more normal now," Stephen said gently. "With that leg you can already walk and hold yourself completely differently, and that will be worth a lot."

At that, Wesley grinned again. "You're not kidding. I'm not trying to be greedy here, but, considering we're talking arms, it would be really nice to get that dealt with too."

"We can start the process, but only if Shane here thinks it's healed enough."

"I don't think it has," he replied. "Neither do I think the time and effort to get that arm where you want it to be is something we should put into a prosthetic at this point. We need to get you stronger first."

Wesley looked over at Shane and frowned, not liking anything he had to say.

Shane nodded. "Otherwise you'll just have to make adjustments afterward as you improve in strength, and those will be costly," he reminded him.

Wesley nodded. "I guess so, … but you're dissing on my dream. You know that, right?"

Shane laughed. "No, I'm not," he argued. "I'm not even postponing it. I'm just putting a realistic restraint on it for the moment. You've got your leg, and, as long as it's good to go, we'll work on strengthening up your related muscles so your walking gait doesn't favor one leg over the other, which right now you are doing," he pointed out to everybody.

"Really?" Wesley asked, looking at him in surprise.

"Yes, you are. So we have that to deal with, and I would just as soon deal with that before we even get started with adjusting your arm strength to account for an arm prosthetic."

Wesley sighed. "Right, so we always have to be the sensible ones."

"It's your body," Shane said. "You want to sore it up and be off the prosthetics again for another what? Four, six, eight weeks, if not months?"

"No, I don't," he stated, "so *fine*. We'll work on it. But Stephen can still do some tests on the nerves and the muscles of my arm today, couldn't he?"

"Absolutely," Shane agreed. "And that's a start."

Stephen nodded. "We've got another forty minutes here," he noted, looking down at his phone. "Then we'll have to call it a day, but we will be back. We do come here on a fairly regular timeframe."

"Good," Wesley said. "Do you guys know a woman named Kat out of New Mexico?"

"Yeah, sure do," Stephen said. "We deal with her all the time."

"Any particular work that you do with her?"

"She has some techniques that are slightly different than ours," he said, looking up from the computer. "And some of her stuff works better for some of our people, and some of hers works better with our style," he added. "It all depends what we have to work with as to who can give you the most mobility," he stated.

"Ah, I guess that makes sense. Never thought of it from that point of view."

"Nope," Stephen agreed. "You're just looking at getting the best deal that you can get for your body, and believe me that we understand that," he said, with a big grin. "That's why we do what we do because, it really brightens our world to see you guys doing so well with our tools and equipment," he murmured. "Now, let's sit down and get through some of this arm testing. Then we'll have to run."

Chapter 11

ALBA LEANED AGAINST the open doorway and watched as the men tested the nerves on the arm stump that Wesley had left. She noted the extra skin flap that covered the ending, the stump, and a little bit extra had been built in so that he could wear something there. She'd also heard Shane tell him to hold back his arm prosthetic a little bit, so that they had time to build up enough strength in that little wing to do what Wesley wanted done with a prosthetic down the road.

And she agreed with Shane, but she saw how hard it was for Wesley to hold back. He was like a kid in a candy store. Somebody had given him a toy he desperately wanted, and now he wanted the moon. The toy he'd had didn't work very well, and what he really needed was a fully functional one. Interesting too that he kept talking about this woman out of New Mexico.

As Shane walked over, Alba murmured, "Who is this Kat person out of New Mexico?"

Shane smiled. "She's a specialist in prosthetics."

"Ah, so he wants to contact her. Is this prosthetic not good enough?"

"We'll find out," he said. "According to these guys, they work with Kat all the time, and it depends on what the situation is, as to which person is better to help the patient."

"Right. Well, he doesn't seem to need me at all today."

"I don't know about that." Shane raised one eyebrow.

"When they're gone, there'll be euphoria, and then there'll be the let-down," she shared, with a nod.

"Got it." Shane nodded.

"In the meantime," she said, "I'll head back to work because they'll be busy here for a while."

"They've got another forty minutes, or"—he looked at his watch—"another thirty minutes max."

"Good enough," she said. "Sounds as if it was still a good day for him."

"I think so," Shane confirmed, studying Wesley in front of them. He was completely engrossed in the questions that the two tech designers were asking.

"It is interesting to see him in this environment. And to see how much he really values these prosthetics."

"I'm just glad that he'll get one today," Shane noted, looking at her.

"I am too," she murmured. "It would have broken his heart if it didn't fit. But it looks good on him."

"Not only looks good on him but he looks as if he's doing really well with it," Shane noted. "Sure, we have a way to go, but I can see that we also have a means to get there."

"And that's what counts." Alba smiled. "We'll get him through this." And, with that, she turned and headed back to her office.

She felt surprisingly teary, and there was absolutely no reason for it. This was good news all around. Wesley had done exactly what he needed to do, and the tech guys had done what they needed to do, and it looked as if a working prosthetic leg was coming Wesley's way today. They would have a fight to get it off him. She grinned at that.

Wesley wanted that sucker, and he wanted it on. But they hadn't taken it off to see if there was any soring up yet, so that could still be a problem today. She hoped not. When she returned to her office, she ended up buried in appointments and the related paperwork.

As she hadn't heard from Wesley by the time dinner rolled around, she slowly got up from her desk and stretched, realizing that she'd been glued to her desk a lot longer than she had expected and even now was looking down at a stack of paperwork still to be done.

She shut off her computers and walked out of her office, locking the door. She yawned again, realizing just how tired she was. The emotional stress had been a killer this week. But she'd also thoroughly enjoyed her time off, something she'd needed. Time and distance always helped, particularly with difficult patients. She walked toward the dining room.

When a shout came from behind her, she turned to see Wesley, walking on two legs toward her, his grin a mile wide.

She stopped and waited for him, delighted that he'd stopped her. "Hey, don't you look fancy."

"It feels great," he said. "Look at me."

"I didn't think you were that tall," she noted in amazement.

"Right? When you're not standing, it's, … it's hard to even imagine height," he muttered.

"I knew you were tall, even seated, but I didn't realize you were over six foot."

He nodded. "My daddy and both my brothers are too." He did a slow turn in front of her.

"And how does it feel?" she asked.

"Better than I expected," he murmured. "I put up with a lot of pain last time in order to keep it because I really wanted it. But, of course, I pushed it too hard, and the end result was I ended up losing it anyway. Plus it set me back."

"So now you know better," she noted gently. "You need to give it time to adapt, use it a little bit, not use it for long stretches of time for a while, and let your body break it in gently."

"I know, and I'll have to be reminded of that on a regular basis," he admitted, "because I won't want to go back to a wheelchair."

"And yet you might find that it's a relief to go back to a wheelchair," she pointed out. "You're using different muscles right now, and those will get sore pretty fast."

"Shane already warned me that we'll work on that tomorrow." He motioned ahead. "After you, m'dear."

She smiled at him and then stepped forward.

He noted, "You're looking really tired."

"I am," she agreed, as she stifled yet another yawn.

"I haven't seen you around for a few days."

She glanced over at him to hear a studied indifference in his tone. "I had days off," she murmured.

"That must have been nice for you, I'm sure," he replied, although his scrutiny had turned intense, as he studied her face. "You look as if you need another few days off."

She burst out laughing. "It's just the work right now. If I take off, the paperwork remains. I have a lot of reports to write, and that just never, ever goes away."

He winced at the term *reports*. "Not my favorite job," he stated.

"No, but the minute you get involved, there's always paperwork that has to be followed up on."

"I guess, but definitely not my favorite job."

She nodded. "I don't mind it mostly, but there are definitely times when I would just as soon find something else much more fun to do," she murmured. They moved forward in line.

"You didn't mention that you were on days off," Wesley said. "I admit that I asked Shane about you a couple times."

"I think you had more than enough of me there for a while," she noted. "It didn't occur to me to tell you because I hadn't seen you right then. And I was not supposed to go out of town, but I got an invitation, so I took it."

"Ah, a girlfriend?"

She looked at him and then nodded. "Yes, a girlfriend." And she watched as the relief crossed over his face. "Would it bother you if it wasn't?"

"I don't have any right for it to bother me," he replied in a wry tone. "Yet I appreciate the fact that there isn't anybody special in your life."

Her lips quirked at that. "I don't know so much about not having anybody special in my life," she teased, with a wry tone. "But the person I do have is definitely difficult."

He stared at her, but just then Dennis called over, "Hey, you two, do you want to keep moving the line forward?"

And that's when they realized they'd allowed a large gap to form between them and the person in front of them.

She walked over and mumbled, "Sorry about that."

"That's all right," Dennis said, with an airy wave of his ladle. "Apparently we have all day to look after you guys."

She rolled her eyes at that. "Okay, that's a bit thick," she teased. Then she saw a Greek salad in front of her. "Oh my," she whispered.

"Yep, it's one of your favorites. I know. So let's get you a big bowl of that, and what do you want to go with it?"

By the time they were done, her plate was overflowing.

"Dennis, you'll make me fat."

"I won't make you nothing," he argued, with a grin, "except for maybe happy."

"I'll take happy," she agreed. "It's amazing just how much the food here goes a long way to keeping everybody's moods up."

"You have to in this place. We are healers, even those of us in the kitchen. Good food is good for the soul, and what we deal with here is a lot of broken souls. We're putting them back together, one plateful at a time." And, with that, he moved on to the next customer.

She picked up the cutlery she needed and looked around the dining room, which was already pretty full. She wasn't even sure whether she should mention about eating together or not. Wesley might want to go off and dine with other people. He had a lot to show off today. And just while she was contemplating where to go and what to say, a couple guys called out to him.

"Hey, let's get a load of those new legs," they called over to him.

She stepped forward and headed out to the deck, even as Wesley walked over to join the men at the table. She didn't even watch to see what happened; she just kept on going. Outside, she set her plate down and refused to look behind her. Her patients got better and flew the coop. It's the way of the world, and she needed to deal with it.

And she had absolutely no reason that she couldn't have joined him—except that the guys hadn't invited her—but there was also no reason that Wesley couldn't have joined her. So she would just let the cards lay where they fell. When somebody sat down beside her, she looked over at Wesley, frowning. "You can go eat with your friends, you know."

"I could," he agreed, "but it was brought home to me in a surprising way that I haven't necessarily treated everybody very well. So I thought maybe we could have dinner together. I'll go down and visit with Stan afterward."

She asked, "What's going on at Stan's?"

"He's got foxes," he declared, with a big grin.

"Foxes?" she repeated. "I don't think we've ever had any here yet, or at least none that I've seen."

"Stan's got … I think he called it a *kit*."

She frowned. "Maybe. So we have babies down there?"

He nodded. "Somebody had a pet fox, and it was due to give birth, but there were a few complications, so they brought it in, and Stan's been looking after it ever since."

"It? Solo?"

"She was due to have babies, but I don't know what happened. I wanted to go down and see what the end result was."

"Sounds good. If you don't mind company, I would like to see it."

He looked at her and smiled. "You know I would like company."

She shook her head, tired of beating around the bush. "I don't know that. We didn't part on great terms last time," she stated. "I've just been giving you space."

"And enough of that," he declared forcibly. "There's space, and then there's space. We didn't even have a real spat. I just got my nose out of joint."

She smiled. "In my world that happens a fair bit."

"You were right to push me," he admitted. "I still am not happy about the delay with the prosthetic arm's progress, and I very much want to get that prosthetic too, but I need a better one than what they offered last time," he shared. "And

I know it sounds as if I'm just asking for more than I can really have, but I'm not so sure about that. I'm not ready to accept less."

"Good, which is why you should keep researching to see what options you have," she pointed out. "Did they have anything to suggest today?"

"Nothing more than what they already had for me, although they had something that was a little more permanent."

"What about the nerves? Did they test the arm for that?"

"Yes," he said, smiling. "And they're coming along. There's still some nerve damage from the surgeries, *blah, blah, blah, blah*."

"In other words, you're not quite ready yet."

He groaned. "No, and that, of course, will just make Shane feel that much better because he's the one who told me to slow down, to hold back, and to wait."

She chuckled. "And I guess you don't like being told to wait, *huh*?"

He shook his head. "No, definitely not. Nothing like an accident like this to make you sit back and take another look at your life and who you are, and what you need to do."

"I dunno," she muttered. "I think you're doing just fine."

He shook his head. "No, I'm not, actually," he admitted. "I'm too impatient. I expect more from others than what they're prepared to give, and, just when I think that I'm doing okay with it, I realize that I've been pushing people away, instead of letting them come closer."

"Sometimes, when we need to hear things, we don't like the message," she shared. "And we tend to blame the messenger. There's a reason that meme became so popular."

He nodded. "I hadn't really seen that I was doing that, but I guess I was." He looked down at the Greek salad on his plate and frowned.

"What? You don't like Greek salad now?" she asked in a teasing tone.

He looked over at her and said, "I love Greek salad. But I have to admit that I owe you an apology."

She raised one eyebrow. "I wasn't expecting that."

"And that's sad too," he murmured, "because just the fact that you weren't expecting it says a whole lot to me. I should have done that as soon as I saw you, but I was holding back," he admitted, "and that's, … that's a problem."

"It's not a problem," she argued gently. "It is what it is. It's not necessarily something to ask forgiveness for, or anything else. You're entitled to your emotions. You're entitled to feel happy, sad, angry, upset. We only get into trouble when we forget that we need to let out these emotions and that honesty is always the best policy."

He settled back, studying her, and replied in a bright tone, "In that case, I have to ask. Did you leave town to get away from me?"

"Oh, interesting," she murmured, staring at him. She looked as if she wanted to say something and then stopped.

"Remember that *honesty is the best policy*," he repeated.

She laughed. "I left to get away from the whole situation. Sometimes, living and working here, with the patients, the staff, and all of us together, with not enough of a break, it can be a bit much," she shared. "So it wasn't necessarily to get away from you but from the situation, the undercurrents, the emotions, the frustrations. Yeah, I needed a break from work," she admitted. She watched his face as she had shared that, and he nodded, as if it confirmed something. "Is that a problem?" she asked.

"No, not at all, and thanks for being honest. I felt terrible when I realized that you were gone, as I had reacted badly to your counsel. So I went to apologize that next morning and to see if you were okay, if *we* were okay," he clarified, "but you'd left, and Shane just didn't say anything—other than you'd gone for your days off."

"I didn't talk to Shane about it," she pointed out. "We have hundreds of staff here, and lots of us are closer than others," she murmured. "But you have to remember that everybody here has lives outside of work, including Shane."

Wesley laughed. "I met his partner," he said, with a bright smile. "He's a lucky man."

"He is, indeed," she noted, with a smile. "And he met her here."

"I heard that, and it sometimes just blows me away."

"Why? Because you don't see yourself as whole?"

He winced. "It keeps coming back to that, doesn't it?"

"Well, you tell me," she said. "Why does it blow you away that he found somebody here?"

"Because Shane is a pretty special guy, and you would think that he could pick and choose and find a very special partner."

"He did," she stated. "What is it that you think is wrong about the scenario?"

"I don't think it's wrong. I think, in their case, they made it work. I'm just not sure that it would work for me."

"Ah, right. So your situation is different because you don't have an arm and a leg."

He slumped in the chair beside her. "Sounds like we're going to fight again."

AND WESLEY HATED that. It made him feel as if he was in the wrong, as if, yet again, he should have done something else to avoid this.

"No," she disagreed gently. "No fighting. It's just an observation. Once again though, it sounds as if you …" And she stopped, as if once again trying to feel her way through the conversation. "As if you're *less than* because you don't have that arm. The leg, you can put on pants, and nobody will see, at least in the initial moment, until they get to know you better. Yet that missing arm is visible."

He nodded slowly. "It is visible," he agreed, as he looked down at it. "And it really hurts me that it's missing."

"And it hurts you emotionally that, in your mind, you're not as good as everybody else because you have this missing limb," she added, her tone incredibly gentle.

He faced her and nodded. "How would anybody accept me, when they could choose somebody who's whole and healthy?"

"When it comes to love and relationships, I think we do less of the *choosing* and more of the *accepting* when it really matters," she shared. "You're perfectly capable of doing an incredible amount of things with the arm as is because you'll find a way to do it because you're motivated to find a way to do something about it," she pointed out. "Other people will see it over time, but it's how you see you. It's got nothing to do with how somebody else sees you. It's all about how *you* see you and whether you can accept yourself with just one arm."

"And if I can't?" he asked, leaning forward with an intensity that unfortunately belied the casualness of his tone.

But it was hard to control given the conversation.

"What do you mean, *if you can't?*"

"What if I can't accept it," he repeated. "What if I can't live with this?"

"The choices are pretty slim," she noted. "And I would seriously hope that you don't mean what you're saying."

He frowned at her and then immediately shook his head. "No, I'm not suicidal," he declared, "but how do I accept me—as is—and not try to constantly make amends or adjustments or whatever in order to be *as good as?*"

"That comes with time and self-love. And that *is* something you *can* accept. It just takes a little bit of effort."

"Will you help me?" he asked, his voice low.

She gripped his fingers with her hand and whispered, "Absolutely. The first thing you have to do is realize that not everybody will judge you as you are judging you. A lot of people won't even notice it. And those who do and reinforce this *less than* feeling in you, they don't matter. They aren't the people who are important to you in life."

"And what about the ones who are important to me?"

"If they love you," she stated, "it won't matter to them either. So you'll need to pick and choose the people in your world because it'll be the people who can accept you as who you are who will be the ones who you want to keep. Everybody else? If they can't? I hate to say it, but it might be time to clean out your friend closet."

He stared at her and nodded. "Would I really get rid of a long-term friendship because they can't accept who I am?"

"Would you really want a long-term friendship with someone who can't accept who you are today?" she countered.

He sat back and stared at her. "No, not really."

"Exactly. It's all about new beginnings in all directions."

Chapter 12

RUE TO ALBA'S word, she spent the next couple weeks, devising exercises and working with Wesley to deal with his lack of self-esteem when it came to his missing arm. She deliberately told several other staff in the center where his issues were at, so that the staff would make a point of noticing his arm and commenting on it, noticing the improvements he had made over the weeks, noticing how he was adapting to it—even without a prosthetic. Some had some interesting prosthetics for him to consider.

This way Alba hoped that Wesley became a little more accustomed to people talking about it, all in the guise of trying to make him feel a little more comfortable just discussing it. It wouldn't be the same as being out in the public because everybody in public didn't have the same training that the staff in this center had. But definitely this was a good start. She also made him a pouch, with a Velcro fastener. When she brought it to his room several days later and held it out, he shook his head.

"What's this?" he asked.

"It's a Velcro pouch, with a strap that goes around your neck," she said. "I stitched it up for you." He frowned at her, and she smiled. "This is a really soft bamboo fabric on the inside." And she reached over and strapped it around his neck and also fastened it onto his little wing. "And it's got a place for your cell phone." She held out her hand, and he put his cell phone in it, and she popped it in. "It's got a pocket to put a few pencils, a couple keys, whatever you want along that line," she added. "And it's got a hook, so you can put something on it. Plus it's got a couple Velcro straps if you want to strap something in." She showed him how it worked.

"Did you figure that out and then make it?"

She nodded. "It's something that might be a little more useful for you in the interim, while you wait for your other prosthetic."

He stared at it in surprise. "I'm really touched. I'm not sure that I want to wear it though," he added cautiously.

She grinned at him. "And I figured that would be your response, but I would very much appreciate it if you would wear it just today, see if it's even useful. If I don't have somebody to try out these things on, I don't know if they'll work."

He stared at her hesitantly.

She nodded. "I know. You don't like the idea. But does it really matter what anybody here thinks?"

"No," he admitted. "Everybody here is dealing with stuff themselves."

"Exactly," she pointedly commented. "So maybe just try it out for yourself and decide for yourself."

He nodded. "Fine, although I'm not sure how useful it would be. Despite my whining, I am quite amazed that you created something like that."

She just raised her hand. "I sew whenever I get a few moments, and it just occurred to me that, at this stage, while you're still trying to get a little more mobile and strengthen up that arm, that something like this might come in handy."

He nodded. "I hadn't even considered that. You're right. So, hey, I'll give it a shot."

"Good." She gave him a big smile. "I'm heading down for breakfast. How about you?"

"Yep, let's go," he said, as he stood up on his prosthetic leg, grinning broadly. "Man, I love these legs." And he walked to her side. "Just knowing that I can stand up as tall as I was meant to be is such an incredible feeling."

She smiled. "I'm really glad that you're enjoying it."

He nodded. "It's foolish, isn't it?"

"No, not at all," she argued, with a laugh. "There's little enough sometimes in our lives that we must enjoy the bit that we do have."

"That's what I was thinking," he agreed. "There always seems to be something going down somewhere that it's nice when it's not in my corner."

At that, she really laughed. "I'm not sure that is exactly the way you should look at things, but I get it. Everybody wants to hope they're not the target."

"And yet sometimes it seems as if we all are targets," he joked.

"And yet it's up to you to turn that around too," she pointed out.

"No lectures right now, Doc. We're having breakfast."

And she smiled because he was getting really good at telling her when she could be a therapist and a professional versus when he just wanted to have personal time with her. And she appreciated that. It might be a challenge having a relationship with him when they did have things to work out constantly, but he had also come a long way in a very short time, and she was proud of him.

She thought about that as they sat down with their re

spective plates and shared, "I don't think I've told you, but I'm really proud of the progress you've made."

He stopped, fork midair, and stared at her.

"I really don't tell you enough if it's that much a shock to hear me praise you," she murmured.

"Well, it is kind of a shock," he confirmed, "not so much that you don't tell me, but I guess I don't expect to hear it. In the navy, it's not as if you get kudos for doing anything," he explained. "You're expected to do your job and to do it well."

"And I guess they don't really work on that whole *positive feedback loop* thing, *huh?*"

"No." He chuckled at that. "And that's okay because I understood exactly what was expected, and I could do the job, and I did it to the best of my ability at all times," he explained. "And it's such an odd thing when somebody does compliment you because you're thinking, *Well, dang, I was just doing my job. What's the big deal?*"

"And of course it's not a big deal to you," she noted. "But I'm also very aware that this life, this work that you're doing, it's very internal, and sometimes it's just nice to know that other people can see your progress."

"You're right," he agreed, as he popped his fork into his mouth. "It is nice to hear, so thanks for that," he replied, with a grin. "And I have come a ways, haven't I? Even Shane says so."

"Good," she declared. "So it seems you've made progress on many fronts."

"Yeah, I don't even know how much longer I have here," he admitted, staring at her. "I suppose I should figure that out."

"Dani will let you know ahead of time," she murmured,

"but I think you still have a couple months."

"Good," he replied. "I still want to see about riding the horses here. Not sure if I need both prosthetics before I can do that. I'll have to ask Shane. Regardless I'm not quite ready to leave yet."

"In that case you're not leaving. … You don't have to go."

"I will whenever the budget runs out," he stated, with a smile, "but I won't go far."

"Yeah? You got plans?" she asked, with a teasing tone.

"Yep." He nodded. "Not only do I have plans but I'll do some retraining in town here."

"Oh, good," she said. "I hadn't heard about these plans before."

"*Naw*, I was kinda waiting to really decide what I want to do, before I brought it up."

"And you figured it out already?" she asked.

"Not really, but I am talking to a couple career counselors today," he shared. "They're coming out here to deal with more than just me, I guess, but there'll be some sessions, and I will talk to them about my plans and see what my options are, see what kind of money there is, see how many years I could get for training and all that. I'm still contemplating ideas."

"That sounds wonderful," she said. "I'm quite relieved to hear that. Not everybody has plans when they're here. Usually the plan is to just get out of here."

He burst out laughing at that. "I'm guilty as charged in a way," he admitted. "The first thing you want to do as soon as you're here is graduate. But you have to graduate *to* something," he noted, "and I still need to work out what that something'll be."

"I like the sound of that. So here's to progress." And she lifted her coffee cup and clinked it with his.

"You don't even seem to be too worried about what I will do."

"I'm not," she said. "I know perfectly well that, whatever you decide to do, you'll be a success. You've just got that kind of personality."

He looked at her in appreciation. "Thanks. Sometimes, when you're in these situations, you're not sure you can do what's required of you."

"Oh, I get it," she said, "and you're not alone in that. Even I sometimes think that I can't do what's required of me."

"Yeah, we don't make life easy on you, do we?" he asked, stopping and looking at her. "We don't think about the staff. We don't think about all the pain that you guys go through in dealing with us, and I'm sorry if we've been less than considerate."

She smiled at him. "It's not your job to be considerate, but to focus on healing," she stated. "Still, being appreciated always helps."

"Yeah, that's a big thing, isn't it?"

"It really is," she murmured. "Everybody's got things on their mind, things to do, places to be, and it's so easy to forget the guy caught in the middle."

"And I don't ever want to be that guy," he declared. "I think life is hard enough without it being harder for people who worked so hard to make life easier."

"Good, then chances are, you won't fit into that group."

He chuckled. "I would hope not, but that doesn't mean that I'm all that good at noticing sometimes."

"Just remember to keep up that appreciation, and I'm

sure you'll do just fine," she said, with a smile.

"You're very forgiving, and you make it look so easy."

She hesitated. "Am I?"

He nodded. "You are. People say things all the time, but, in your case, I think you really mean it."

"I do," she said. "I would think everybody here does."

"Maybe," he replied. "I don't have to deal with everybody. Shane is a huge part of my world—and you of course—but outside of you two and maybe a couple others, I don't deal with a whole lot of the actual staff here," he noted. "In a way, it's too bad because I'm sure other very special people are here that I would enjoy meeting, but there's also only so many I can keep track of and can work with at the same time."

She laughed. "Otherwise it's information overload."

"And emotional overload," he added. "When you add one more person to your world, you're also adding their hopes and their dreams and their wishes and their likes and dislikes," he explained. "So you have to add people carefully."

"Is this because you've been discarding other people, as we talked about?"

He looked at her and shrugged. "I hate to see it as a *discard*," he began, "but I've certainly been thinking about who and what I've been calling a friend. And realizing that a lot of the people I would have claimed were friends just aren't. I haven't had anything to do with them in years, and even now I don't feel as if I could necessarily pick up the phone and call them because so much time's gone by."

"Right, so then they're not necessarily friends."

"Exactly, and, if they're not friends, then I put them into the acquaintance category, and that's a whole different story because it means I would have to get to know who they are again. And I have to actually want to do that."

"Which you don't really want to do right now, is that it?"

"Right, that's not my focus right now," he said, with a smile. "I'm still trying to deal with all the rest of this stuff happening."

She laughed. "And there's no pressure to do it now either."

"You're right. I was looking at all these people who, I thought, were *friends*, and a couple in particular who, once they found out about my accident, even though they were also in the navy, I wouldn't consider my friends now," he admitted, "because, let's just say, they didn't respond positively."

"And sometimes," she replied, with a slight warning, "you have to understand that they don't know how to treat you. You're now the one who has changed," she pointed out, "and not everybody's good with change. Yet nobody gets away without having some changes in their lives."

"That's an early lesson, isn't it?" he asked, with a smile. "When you have a major accident, you need somebody out there who warns you that everybody sees you now as something other than human."

"That sounds a bit harsh," she noted, "yet definitely you've changed. You're now injured, and that is a condition all on its own."

"I prefer to say *able-bodied*," he corrected.

"I like that too," she agreed. "So many people here are used to it, so much so that, if we see people in town on crutches or in a wheelchair, it doesn't bother us. Yet, for many other people, they see mostly the crutches or the wheelchair. Those people have never encountered such injuries as that and don't know what to do with that. Most of the time they feel embarrassed because they want to actually see what you have for an arm, but they know that they can't do it without staring, so then they keep casting these furtive glances to try and get a better look."

"And yet wouldn't it be nice if they would just say, *Hey, can I take a close look at your arm?*"

"If that happened to you, what would you say?" she asked curiously.

"I don't know. It's never happened," he stated, with a smile. "But, if I thought I could get a normal response from people, maybe it wouldn't be so bad. Maybe if I had a Kat design, I would want to show it off."

"True." She had to smile at that.

As it was, an incident happened later that week that made everybody in the center stop, and, in her case, smile. She walked out to the front lobby to see a family waiting to visit with a resident here. She smiled at them, as she moved into Dani's office. "Wow, that waiting room is full."

"Yeah, they're here to see Benji," Dani shared.

As Alba stood here in the doorway, she cast another glance at the family and noted that the little girl didn't have an arm. She was carrying a booklet under her one arm and chatting away to her mother. "Oh, that's nice to see," Alba said.

Dani came to the door, took one look, and then nodded. "Right? That tyke was born that way, so it's an easier adaptation. But it'll never be easy," she murmured.

"No, you're right," Alba agreed. "Now, if we could get Wesley up to that level of self-confidence, up to the level of this little girl, we would be doing just fine."

"Maybe you should call him down and have him see her."

"I don't know if that would be a benefit or not," Alba replied. "I suspect that he would be both upset and happy."

As it was, Wesley walked down the hallway on his prosthetic, busy looking at his e-tablet. When he looked up and saw her, he headed to her. "Hey, I came to talk to the admin because I'm having trouble with my e-tablet here." He held it up, looked around at the waiting room, and his gaze landed on the little girl.

The little girl looked up at him, beamed, put down her book, and raced over to him. "You look just like me," she cried out.

He stared at her and then slowly nodded. "You know something? I think I do. Although maybe I'm luckier than you," he added and pointed to his leg.

She stared at it in fascination. She looked up and asked, "Could I touch it?"

"Sure," he said. He looked at her missing arm. "What happened to your arm?"

"My arm? Oh, nothing. This is the way God made me."

From Dani's office, Alba watched the conversation and saw almost the physical blow to Wesley's heart when the little girl had said that. Alba walked over casually and joined the conversation. "Hey, I hear you're here to see Benji, your dad."

She looked up and smiled. "Did you see his leg?" she asked in that same chatty voice, pointing at Wesley's new prosthetic. "Isn't that cool?"

"It is cool, and he'll get something for his arm too, but it won't be anywhere near as cool as that."

The little girl nodded. "I have a couple at home. I don't

really like them though."

Wesley asked in a soft tone, "Why not?"

"Because they don't work. They're okay," she muttered. "Sometimes I wear them when we go out to stop people from staring, but, most of the time, I don't care enough," she said, with a shrug. "People stare anyway."

"And does it bother you?"

She shook her head. "Nope, it doesn't bother me. My friends don't care," she shared, "and my family doesn't care. They love me just the way I am."

He chuckled. "Sounds like you have a special family."

She looked up at him. "Doesn't your family love you the way you are?"

Such sorrow filled her tone, probably expecting Wesley to give her the wrong answer, and she would burst into tears for him. He gazed at her and shook his head. "My family loves me just the way I am."

"Good then," she replied, "so it doesn't matter, does it?"

And, with that, one of the nurses called out to the family, and her mother said, "Annabelle, come on."

Annabelle waved and said, "Bye." Then she raced after her mom.

Wesley turned and looked at Alba. "Dear Lord, talk about messages from the angels."

And then obviously shaken, he turned and slowly walked back to his room.

IN HIS ROOM, Wesley sat down on the edge of the bed, almost consumed with what he had just heard and seen. Why had it taken him so long to understand, and yet that little girl got it right away? Then again, she was living with that missing arm, living with the outcome of how God had made her. He loved that phrase, loved that she was totally okay with the way she was. Obviously there were times when she would have gotten frustrated or angry or upset, but she didn't let it hold her back.

Yet Wesley couldn't see that it was just one challenge. He still had his full faculties. He could still walk. He could still function in so many ways, and yet it had taken a little one-armed girl in the waiting area, asking if she could look at his leg and could touch his prosthetic for Wesley to see the naturalness of what she looked like. And her joy when she saw somebody else who looked like her. They were a minority in this world and a minority that he hadn't asked to be a part of, but now that he was here, he had absolutely no reason to be ashamed of it. He let out a heavy sigh. "What a fool," he murmured.

"Want to talk about it?" Alba asked.

He looked up to see her standing at the doorway. He smiled a little ruefully. "Nothing really to talk about," he muttered. "I just need to process."

"Processing's good."

"Annabelle's adorable, isn't she?" he asked.

"She is, indeed," Alba murmured. "Her dad's a patient here."

"Ah, and will her dad look like her too?"

"Yeah. When I was talking to Dani, she mentioned that her father lost an arm and both legs."

"*Right*," Wesley noted, with a wince. "That would probably help them both bond very well together."

She nodded. "When you think about it, that little girl can help her dad a lot. Help him to adjust. Help him to see who he is now."

"She's good at that," he admitted. "I feel like such a fool." That confession burst out of him. "I've been sitting here, whining about my missing arm, and she's had just one arm for all her life. And you know how mean schoolkids are."

Alba nodded slowly. "They can be brutal," she agreed. "Any group can be, but they don't have to be."

"Right, and she wears her arm sometimes when they go out," he shared, "but most of the time she can't be bothered."

"Meaning that, in other words, she's already adjusted, and, if people have things to say that she doesn't like to hear, she ignores them."

He smiled and nodded. "That's an attitude I need to cultivate."

"It *is* one you're cultivating," she pointed out, with a bright smile. "You just aren't aware of it yet, but you'll be fine."

"I guess," he replied. "And every time I feel sorry for myself, all I need to do is picture Annabelle."

She laughed. "Well, I'm glad Annabelle came today then. Seems it was a worthwhile visit from our perspective, even if not from yours."

"Oh, it was a worthwhile perspective on mine too," he declared. "If nothing else, it's a reality shake-up that I needed."

"Good," she whispered.

As she went to walk away, he asked, "Hey, you up for going to the pool later tonight? I feel as if I need to go."

"Sure, anytime. Maybe just buzz me when you want to meet up."

"Sounds good—and thanks."

She turned to smile at him. "You know that you don't need to say thanks, right?"

"Maybe not," he replied, "but, right now, it feels very much as if I do need to say thanks. So I might overdo it for a while, but it's, again, a process."

She smiled. "In that case, it's all good."

Chapter 13

LATER THAT EVENING, as Alba walked to the pool, after arranging a time to meet Wesley, she stopped to look up at the sky. From the pool she heard Wesley call out to her. She pointed up and said, "A storm's coming."

"Good, hopefully some rain comes with it. We could use it."

"Yeah, you're right there. It's definitely been a little bit too dry."

"It's always dry," he noted, and then he yawned.

She looked at him. "Sounds as if you've had a full day."

"I think it's the emotions as much as anything," he admitted. "Who would've thought meeting a little girl would send my feelings off the wall?"

Alba chuckled. "Annabelle was quite a sweetheart, wasn't she?"

"Yeah," he agreed, with a sigh. "Just one of those sweethearts, with some pretty powerful messages."

"That's how angels come," she agreed, with a gentle smile.

He nodded. "I just hadn't really noticed before, but I got the message this time. ... Come on in and enjoy the water. It's a beautiful evening, at least for the moment."

"If the storm breaks overhead, and it gets ugly, we'll have to get out."

"That's okay. All the more reason for you to get in here soon."

And, with that, she dropped her towel and stepped into the water and dove under. When she surfaced, he was floating alongside her. "You've become quite adept in here."

"Right. Now I want to see Annabelle in here and see what she does."

"You know something? I'm sure she'll move through the water like a dolphin," Alba guessed, "if not a porpoise, if not a fish. There'll always be somebody like her out there to show you the way."

"But you don't always get the message that easily," he noted, with a good-natured complaining tone.

"And you have to recognize the message when it comes," she added, laughing. "In this case you got the message."

"Wow, did I ever. If I thought you had set that up, I would be mad, but I know you didn't."

"No, I sure didn't. And I wouldn't have set it up," she stated. "However, if arranging to talk to somebody else who's missing an arm would have given you that paradigm shift in your viewpoint, I would have done it in a heartbeat."

He smiled. "And like so many others in this place, you're very good about doing what you need to do for others."

"It's why I'm here," she said. "Helping you to adapt, to adjust, to become the best you can be. How could I do anything less?"

"Not everybody's quite so selfless," he noted. "Not everybody is quite so willing to step out and to do more than is required."

"It's not *more* than is required, but it is nice that I can do something to help. Not everybody wants to help others. Not everybody is here to be with somebody," she noted. "However, it's nice when you get an opportunity to help somebody turn on that lightbulb."

He chuckled. "And there we go again because I'm part of that lightbulb comment, aren't I?"

"Let's just say you had a lightbulb that needed turning on," she said, with a smile. "And thankfully Annabelle came by today as an angel in disguise."

He nodded as he kicked gently, floating alongside her.

"Just look at yourself now," she said. "You're so relaxed in the water, so comfortable, and it's a far cry from the way you started."

"At the time, I was petrified I would sink and afraid I would never swim again."

"And it's all about just getting comfortable in the new reality," she murmured.

He nodded. "Like so many other things in life," he added.

"It's all about accepting the changes that are happening and adapting," she said, "being flexible, seeing what comes up, what happens, and going with it."

"After the emotional hit I got earlier today, I should sleep well tonight," he shared. "Just so many emotions were involved today. And releasing all those emotions wore me out."

"It can be harder than anything," she said. "Just knowing that all those emotions are flowing can make life pretty special. It can also be a catalyst to other changes, other things that you need to accept, other issues in your life that you hadn't been quite ready to look into."

He looked at her and rolled his eyes. "Not sure I have too much more I can deal with," he replied, "at least not tonight."

"Oh, don't worry about it," she said, her smile even brighter. "Just think about it. Once you open that door, so many things can happen. But not today, not tonight," she repeated. "You get a reprieve and a chance to assimilate this new you."

"Good. In that case I'm almost ready to call it quits."

Just then came a clap of thunder overhead.

She laughed. "Time for us to go anyway." She waited until he got out and got into his wheelchair and asked, "No leg tonight?"

"No, I didn't want to put all that stuff back on. So it was all about just getting down here and enjoying the water."

"Good, that sounds like progress too, knowing when *not* to wear the prosthetic."

He laughed, and, as he slowly wheeled away, he called out, "Have a good night."

"You too," she murmured, smiling as if she hadn't smiled in a very long time.

When progress happened, it was special, and, when progress happened to somebody you cared about, it was beyond special. And, with that, she headed back to her apartment on the property, a bright smile still on her face.

WESLEY SLEPT BETTER last night, to put it mildly. When he got up the next morning, everything felt relaxed, almost settled, in his mind. Such an odd feeling, and he didn't even care to put his leg on because he knew that he would be doing a ton of exercises with Shane later. So Wesley hopped into his wheelchair, ready to roll down to breakfast. As he went to leave his room. he remembered the pouch that Alba had sewn for him, and he rolled back inside, secured the pouch in place, tucked in his cell phone, adding his notepad and a pen because he always wanted to jot down notes. He admired the fact that the pouch was as useful as it was and then rolled his way toward the dining room.

As he got in line, Dennis looked up at him. "Bright and early this morning."

"Yep," Wesley said, "and hungry."

"Good man." Dennis gave him a big smile. "Go grab a table."

"I wanted to get food first."

"You have to wait a moment," he said, "unless you're hungry right now."

"No, I could grab a coffee first. I didn't realize I was that early."

"It's not even so much that you're early, but we're just a few minutes behind getting everything out. So grab a table, and I'll bring you a plate over."

"Sure. Sounds good."

And, with that, Wesley headed out onto the deck in the early morning sun, pulled out his notepad and pen and jotted down all the thoughts that had been running through his head, and, boy, were there a lot. He wrote down as much as he could remember about the fateful encounter with Annabelle, not wanting to look back later and wish that he had written more down at the time.

When Dennis came by with coffee, he noted, "You forgot to grab coffee on your way."

He looked at it and shook his head, "Man, I must have been seriously not awake yet."

"Maybe." Dennis studied the pouch on his arm. "Wow, I really like that."

Wesley nodded and grinned. "Yeah, my dearly beloved doctor made that for me."

"That's really cool," Dennis said, "and very helpful."

"You're not kidding," Wesley noted, with a smile. "Alba has been surprising me over and over again."

"She's quite the woman. Go you." And, with that, he headed back to get breakfast.

Wesley realized how it meant everybody around them saw them as a twosome. And yet it wasn't anything he had broached with her yet. Neither had she asked what he would do when he left, although she had tentatively brought up the subject yesterday. He hadn't really been forthcoming because he was still working on his plan. He'd had a couple ideas come up but hadn't really thought about them too much, not yet at least. He was a little bit further off than he wanted to be from some of these plans, but, hey, it was one of the things that he just had to sit down and spend some time working on, and maybe go back to school for. He wasn't sure yet. As he sat here, staring off in the distance, Alba called out to him. He turned to look at her and waved her over. "Hey, good morning."

"Good morning," she said. "How are you doing this morning?"

"Good, more determined, more at peace—that's the word I'm looking for. I feel more at *peace* than I was before."

"That's excellent," she said, as she sat down beside him.

"I was also thinking," he began.

And then Dennis appeared out of the blue.

Wesley looked at the plateful of food that Dennis put down in front of him and said, "I am so going to miss your cooking when I'm not here."

"Are you leaving anytime soon?" he asked.

"Nope, I'll drag it out as long as I can."

Dennis burst out laughing. "Nope, just like everybody else, you'll be anxious to leave as soon as you can," he corrected, "and that's just the way of the world."

"I guess," Wesley agreed, "but I'll miss you guys."

"It depends how far away you go," Dennis stated. "They're starting to do inhouse day-training for people who are close by, who come back for refreshers on some of their exercises."

Wesley stared at him. "That is an excellent idea. I'm not even out of here, and I want to get signed up."

"Well, you know who to talk to, as those projects are one of Shane's babies."

"I will do that," he said, as Dennis left. He looked over at Alba. "No breakfast?"

"I'll get something," she said.

And there was that serene smile on her face again.

Chapter 14

ALBA DIDN'T KNOW what to say.

"You get that look on your face," Wesley said intuitively, "when you hear something that you're trying not to react to."

She stared at him over her coffee cup.

"And now you've got that look that says, *How do you respond without giving away what's going on?*" he added. "And it always comes up—or at least let me say this. I've noticed it coming up a couple times whenever we talk about me leaving."

"Of course I'm not happy you're leaving, but, like Dennis just mentioned, it's the way of the place."

"I'm not going far."

"When you say that, I'm delighted to hear it. I'm still not exactly sure what *far* is yet."

"And I'm not sure either. I sent off some inquiries yesterday," he murmured. "And I'm still a way away from figuring out just what to do. And the idea is a little bit on the far-fetched side, so I'm not sure."

"You want to give me any hints?"

He looked at her and smiled. "Well, kinda. It's because of you that I started this. So I probably should give you some hints but, I'm just … I'll just warn you that nothing's for sure, okay?"

"Got it. So what are all these big plans?"

He shrugged. "I contacted the local community college."

"Oh? What will you take?"

"I explained my situation and was wondering if there was any chance of teaching shop."

She stared at him for a long moment. "Wow!" she exclaimed. "When you make a change, you make a change."

"I only did this yesterday," he reminded her, "after meeting Annabelle."

"Ah, because of how relaxed she is about her arm."

"It just reminded me that I was a fool and an idiot and that I was hiding and that, if she wasn't hiding, there was no reason I should be hiding," he shared. "As I mentioned yesterday, seeing her was quite the eye-opener."

"I like it. Have you had a response?"

"No, and honestly, I'm not even sure that any response would be one that I would like—because obviously I'm not as able-bodied as I once was."

"And did you tell them that?"

"Not only told them but I sent them a photo of the injuries and told them that I was perfectly capable of doing a lot of things that I needed to do and that some of the machines I needed to adapt to, but I wondered if they had a program for people like me to learn skills and hobbies or if they did any training, any hands-on technical-type training, for handicapped people."

"Oh, that's a fascinating idea," she exclaimed, staring at him. "I really like it. When you hear back from them, let me know."

"Oh, I will," he promised. "And now, go get food," he ordered. "We don't have much time before our day starts. And you know what that can be like."

She burst out laughing and got up. "Aye-aye, captain. See you back here in a few minutes."

AMAZING JUST HOW much freer Wesley felt, after having met that little girl, Annabelle. Stupid, yes, like an idiot, an adult who had missed a major learning curve somewhere along the line and had to be shown by a small angel. He almost wished he could see the little girl again and thank her. But she probably wouldn't even understand because to her it was natural, it was normal. He's the one who had made a big deal out of nothing. And that had just complicated his issue.

He could still feel himself adjusting, depending on his thought processes. He would be sitting in the dining room and looking around and suddenly realize that he wasn't feeling the same sense of judgment anymore. And he didn't know if that was coming from the people around him or if that was self-induced, but, because of that lack of judgment, he had so much more freedom. It was stupid. It was ridiculous, and it was a number of other feelings that he was more than happy to let go of.

When he heard from the local community college, he stared at the email reply. He hadn't even expected to get a response. As he read the message, he was even more stunned. They wanted to talk with him, see what his capabilities were, and see what he had in mind. He immediately responded, replying how that would be perfect and what time frame were they looking at for a meeting. As it was, they went back and forth with several emails, confirming the time and the date, and then he realized that he didn't have any way to get into town.

And then he got an email from Kat. He froze, not sure he wanted to read it, but he did. *Send me your medicals*, she said, *and I'll be in touch*.

He sat here, staring at the emails, with a frown on his face, only to have a knock on the door, and Shane poked his head around and asked, "Ah, so were you planning on working out today?"

Wesley stared at him in shock, stared down at the time on his computer. "Oh, man, I am sorry." He got up from the bed and headed in Shane's direction.

"I hope you have a good reason," Shane stated in the testiest tone that Wesley had heard yet from Shane.

"Maybe, at least for me. I don't know about for you." As they walked down to the therapy room, Wesley explained.

Shane stared at him. "Seriously?"

Wesley nodded. "I don't know what I was thinking," he admitted, wincing. "I'm hardly to that point yet."

"No, but that likely isn't something they'll want to start on Monday anyway," Shane pointed out. "So, if this is something that's doable, we need to figure out a way to ensure that you're capable of doing the job."

"That's what I don't know," Wesley admitted. "And I don't really have any machinery to practice on."

"No," Shane replied slowly, "but we have a workshop here because things always need to be repaired around here."

Wesley stared at him. "You have a workshop?"

"Sure. It's down in the basement," he noted. "Not a ton of equipment is there either, but obviously drills and circular saws and handsaws." He added, "I don't even know what all else is down there. However, I can call one of the mainte-nance men and see what we can set up."

Wesley stared at Shane. "That would be an incredible

opportunity, if for no other reason than to test what I can do and what I want to do."

"And considering you've already reached out to the college, maybe we should do that now."

Wesley winced at that. "Yeah, that would be a good idea."

Shane nodded. "Today we'll work on strengthening that arm. In the meantime I will see what I can work out with the workshop. Even if we can get an hour or so to test and to see what you need to do, that would be a start."

And, with that, the morning progressed at the same speed that it had started. And by the time lunch came around, Wesley was now onto another problem in his head. He needed to talk to Dani to see if he could get a ride into town to visit the college. He knew that people went in for shopping trips and day trips and various things to keep them socially active and aware, but this was a completely different thing. He would probably have to pay for a round-trip visit, probably have the driver waiting for Wesley in the interim. But it would be worth it, if it resulted in something positive.

"Heck," he muttered to himself. "It is positive already."

The bottom line was somebody had expressed interest, without dismissing him as having nothing to offer. He was still preoccupied with that thought, when Alba sat down beside him at lunch.

"Hey," she greeted him. "What's with the expression on your face?"

He looked at her, blinked to bring his mind back to it, and said, with a wry look, "You won't believe what happened."

She stared at him for a moment. "Well, from the tone of your voice, you're quite nonplussed about it, so tell me."

He explained about the multiple emails, missing out on Shane's workout time frame, and Shane's offer to contact maintenance to see what there was for tools here so that they could test how Wesley could handle various implements. She put down her fork, interlocked her fingers together, and dropped her chin on them, as she stared at him. "When you get moving, you get moving."

He laughed. "I wasn't expecting anybody to get moving with me though," he noted in a wry tone.

"Yeah, you're back to that, *Hey, I can't do this*."

"No," he corrected. "I'm back to, *Oh my God, can I do this?*"

"I'll take that as a huge step forward," she declared, "and that's absolutely fabulous."

He nodded. "Yeah, I have to talk to Dani next though."

"And why is that?" she asked.

"Because I don't know how I would begin to get to town for this."

She shrugged. "Depending on how you feel about it, I could take you."

He stared at her. "Seriously?"

"Sure, why not?" she asked. "I do go to town, not all that often, but it's not a hardship for me to do."

"But it would be during work hours," he noted cautious-ly.

"And I have lots of breaks in my hours where I do re-ports," she reminded him. "I can certainly take you in, and something like this would definitely be part of my job, or at least isn't a hard stretch to consider as part of my job," she explained. "Getting you out there to meet somebody who has a potential career path for you?" she exclaimed. "That would be *huge*." She added, "Not to mention a significant boost to your self-confidence."

"Yeah, but would … How will I feel in front of multiple able-bodied people?"

"And how would you feel in front of others who are *not* able-bodied people?" she asked, tilting her head to study his face. "Because you have to wonder that maybe there's an awareness that something like this is needed for the community at large, for those who don't have the same physical abilities as others—maybe the elderly, maybe the youth."

"Well, that would be even better," he replied, staring at her. "But I doubt the college is running something like that, and, in that case, even if they are, it would probably only be a night class or two."

"It's not a bad way for you to start though," she noted. "What an *in* that would give you."

He had to nod. "It's still"—he stopped and winced—"scary."

"Of course it is," she agreed. "It would be scary no matter what you were doing. But, in this case, you'll be utilizing your ability to your advantage."

"Is that … what's the term?" he asked. "Like maybe *abusing* my ability?"

She stared at him, shook her head slowly, and asked, "Still some more judgments you have to get rid of, *huh?*"

He nodded. "Yeah, apparently, but I'm working on it."

"You are, indeed, and you're doing a great job," she murmured.

He laughed. "You're a great cheerleader."

"I'm more than that," she declared, with a smile. "And did they give you some time frame when they wanted to talk to you?"

He nodded. "They suggested this Monday," he replied

nervously.

She let out her breath in a slow exhale. "Wow, that's amazing. Monday morning?"

He nodded.

"Well, you're in luck," she said. "Monday mornings are generally slow for me, and I can shuffle a few things around to make it happen. And that's only if you're okay for me to go with you."

"I would rather you went with me," he replied, "because, if I completely muck it up and make a fool out of myself, I would just as soon not have too many eyes and ears around to hear about it."

"Just mine," she said, with a smile.

"But you won't judge me for it," he stated. "You'll give me one of those big pep talks on the way home and tell me to try again."

At that, she burst out laughing. "You're so right there, and glad to hear that you know who I am."

ALBA COULDN'T EVEN begin to express how amazed and how proud she was of Wesley's progress. Once he'd seen how he was letting something emotional and physical, yet superficial, affect his life, he'd made changes in a drastic way. She had no clue what the college had in mind, and she didn't think Wesley did either. She quickly did a Google search to see if they did have shop classes for the handicapped, but they didn't appear to—although they did certain things for less able-bodied persons than others. She frowned at that, not wanting to interfere but hoping that would be something that Wesley had a good experience from. If it was a good experience, then he would continue to stretch and to try new things. But, if it went south, well, she wouldn't blame him for wanting to pull back inside his shell again.

WHEN MONDAY MORNING dawned clear, Alba knew Shane and Dahl were waiting on tenterhooks, the same as Alba was, but she walked out to the car with Wesley and pointed hers out.

"Nice. Is the AC on?"

"Not yet," she said, with a laugh. She got in, adjusted

her seat, and turned on the AC, as he got in beside her. "There you go. Now you've got AC."

He just grinned. "So, depending on how long this takes," he said, "I was thinking we might have lunch in town."

She looked over at him in surprise. "I was thinking the same thing."

"Oh, good."

As they drove in, she noted, "The college isn't very far away."

"I know," he murmured. "I was thinking about that too. Wondering if there was something I could do now while I'm still healing and work at building up my strength and maybe do more a little bit later."

"Just don't try to push it," she reminded him.

He grinned at her. "No, that wasn't really on my plan, but I'm eager to get back to whatever I can get back to."

She nodded. "I like the sound of that."

When they pulled up into the parking lot of the college, she turned off the engine and looked at him. He just sat here, staring at the building. He let out a slow, deep breath and turned to face her. "It's not foolish," he stated, "yet a part of me says this is really foolish."

"And that part doesn't matter," she declared. "We're here, and you'll go through with this, and we'll see just what options they have for you. And it's not just them. There are government programs, all kinds of opportunities out there for you."

He nodded. "Yeah, I was thinking of that too," he admitted. After a big sigh, he added, "Well, nothing ventured, nothing gained." He looked at her and added, "This will also sound foolish, but I was hoping I could go in alone."

"Doesn't sound foolish at all," she agreed. "I'll go sit in that beautiful set of gardens over there. You can find me when you're done."

He nodded. "Good enough." And he opened the door and hopped out.

She watched as he walked straight and tall in through the front doors. She also noted he had no limp. Whatever adjustments they had made to the prosthetic, and/or whatever Shane had done to correct the balance in his stride seemed to have worked. He will not be as sore when he got home at the end of the day. Either way, he had presented himself as a very able-bodied male.

She'd heard from Shane that they'd spent a lot of time over the weekend, extra time for Shane but, because of the Monday deadline, he'd been happy to do it, set out in the maintenance room and with two of the maintenance guys who'd also come in and who had worked with multiple machines. Some of the machines were easier to handle, like a sander, and he just had to do things more and more with one hand.

They had utilized her Velcro pouch in another way and had put the cords through it so that he could keep the electrical cords from getting tangled, and he could move them as he wanted to. And she'd found that fascinating. Obviously there'd been some frustration, as he'd had to switch in and out sandpaper and deal with buckles and clips and screwdrivers. The drill had been easy, until it came to removing the bit, but then he'd quickly popped it under his wing and had changed out the bits easily enough too.

By the time he was done with getting more comfortable with those machines, he'd moved on to the circular saw. The handsaw had been fun, and he'd had enough strength to hold a board with his little wing stump when bent over, pressing downward, so that he could actually handsaw. And then the guys had shown him the vise, and he'd gone to town with that. All in all, by the time they'd worked themselves into a sweat, Wesley had been beaming with success. The guys had also been impressed.

Shane had told her, "He can do so much. I'm wondering if we shouldn't incorporate some shop lessons for any of the people who want to just even do basic handyman stuff around the house again."

"I think," she murmured to him, "a lot of guys would want their hobbies back again, and, if this is something that they want to do, even for those who have two able arms, I think it would be a good thing for them to gain self-confidence again."

And, with that, the two of them had gone to Dani.

She'd listened intently, when she'd seen the photos of how well Wesley had done and had heard their stories. She was amazed. "The maintenance room is pretty big, I don't know that it'll pass any safety codes though."

They both winced, as they stared at her.

"Let me look into it," she said. "We might take one room and just section it off and have a big worktable and some tools. As long as they're under supervision at all times ..." She had now focused in on the problem and started jotting down notes.

Alba walked around the college garden, enjoying the beautiful display, realizing that they had a landscape program here as well. All those kinds of things made a difference to the world around you that you didn't even think about. It took people to weed and mow and trim and cut and keep everything in check all the time. And she, for one, rarely found the time to stop and smell the roses. Something else that she needed to do more of.

She shook her head at that because she always had just so much on her mind that she should do. And even now she was worried about Wesley, when there was no need. She knew he would do fabulously. However, it didn't mean that this would be the be-all and end-all, and then he would walk away with a job.

She heard a shout behind her. She turned and watched as Wesley walked toward her. She checked her watch and realized he'd been gone almost an hour. She shook her head at that.

"What are you shaking your head for now?" he teased.

"How much time went by," she replied. "You were in there for an hour, and I didn't even notice. I was just sitting here, enjoying the gardens."

"And that's what they're meant for," he noted, with a serious tone.

"So, how did it go?" She studied his facial expression, looking for any answers. When his face split into a huge grin, she said, "Wow, I'll take that as meaning it went well."

WESLEY LAUGHED. "IT went better than I expected was possible," he admitted. "Obviously there are still some things to work out, but it would be a case of working with the other shop teachers for some of the special needs kids and with the regular students, depending on the projects," he said. "They are looking for a shop teacher. I do need to have certain skills. I do need to have certain certificates, but I don't need to have a degree, although I do have one, which they were happy about. So there is a list of certifications that I would need to get ahead of time, such as first aid, shop safety, and things like that."

She stared at him. "So did they offer you a job?"

"The job starts in January's term," he stated. "Their current shop teacher is leaving for a sabbatical. So they're quite willing to give this a try for the one semester."

"One semester is better than nothing," she said in amazement. "That's absolutely huge news."

"Yeah, I'm feeling pretty cheeky about it," he noted, with a big grin.

"And when do you need to have whatever they want you to have by?"

"The sooner, the better," he replied, "but they're okay if I'm certified by, say, October. They would like to see progress, and, if I change my mind, they would want to know because they, of course, need to have somebody they can count on for the rest of the term."

"Yes, of course," she agreed, shaking her head. "Wow, I'm stunned."

"*Right?*" he said. "So am I, honestly. It's not what I expected. I thought they would send me on my way with the standard line, *We'll consider our options and let you know.* Who would've thought they would offer me the job on the spot?"

"Exactly. Sometimes when it's *not* what you would expect, that is the best thing ever."

"That would definitely qualify in this case," he said. He walked toward the car with her.

"And it's a beautiful place to work," she noted.

He nodded. "And it is close to Hathaway, so, if I sign up for Shane's outpatient workout in the evenings and/or weekends, whatever he decides to set up," he shared, "I was thinking that would be something I would need to do more on a long-term basis, just to keep some of my skills flowing in the right direction."

"Oh, I'm certain anything along that line will be a big help regardless," she noted, "but honestly I'm still stunned." She sat in the car, stared at him, and muttered, "*Wow*." She started the engine. while he watched her.

"You really are happy, aren't you?"

"Of course I am," she declared. "This is sheer amazement. You've done so well."

"And I would be … staying close."

"Oh, don't worry," she said, shooting him a bright grin. "I got that message."

"And, with all this happening," he began, "it did occur to me that I needed a little bit of clarification on something else."

"Shoot," she said, glancing at him as she pulled out into traffic. "And, by the way, are you okay with having lunch in town?"

"Yep, sure am," he said. "A really good burger place is around here."

She laughed. "Ilse's food is always so good, yet she never really does hamburgers, does she? So a messy old-fashioned diner burger sounds good to me." She drove along the road and noted, "It's not even far from here."

He watched as she navigated traffic with competence, realizing that driving would be one of the challenges he had to face. "I'll have to get recertified for driving, won't I?"

"I'm not sure," she replied, looking over at him. "Dani can help you with that."

"Right. And I guess it's really only a matter of having a

simple prosthetic to grab the wheel."

"Maybe, but I don't even think you need that. I think there are adaptations that you can use. You have full functionality of your dominant arm and hand, so maybe it's not a big deal at all."

"It won't be," he declared, and such confidence filled his words that even he laughed. "Listen to me," he said. "This is progress that I wouldn't even have thought was possible a few months ago. And I owe that to you."

"Oh no, you don't," she argued. "You owe that to yourself."

"Do you really believe that?" he asked, eyeing her intently.

"Absolutely I believe that. Hathaway House is a package deal, but the biggest participant in all of it is you," she declared. "You're the one who has to show up. You're the one who has to do the exercises. You're the one who has to do the therapy, and you're the one who has to make the strides forward," she pointed out, "and you have done that in spades. I'm really so proud of you."

He felt his heart warming at that because he knew that she meant it, every word. There wasn't anything false or fake about her. That was one of the reasons he had fallen in love with her; he just hadn't told her that yet.

When they pulled into the parking lot of the diner, she unhooked her seat belt and asked, "Shall we?"

He hesitated and then spoke. "One of the things that I wanted to bring up, regarding the whole *staying close* thing is—" Then he stopped, winced. "I've come a long way, but this is still hard."

"That's fine," she said, twisting in her seat to look at him. "Take as long as you like."

"That's one of the reasons why I'm staying close," he began. "I am trying to take as long as I like and hopefully as long as you like."

She frowned, staring at him. "Sorry?"

He smiled, picked up her hand in his, and drew in a big breath. "I don't want to lose you," he said. "I don't want to move so far away that we can't see each other."

Her fingers closed around his, and she nodded. "I'm really glad to hear that because I feel the same way."

"And I know you feel the same way to a certain extent," he replied hesitantly, "but I'm hoping that you feel the same way to a much greater degree."

Her eyes opened wide. "And to what *greater degree* are you saying?" she asked hesitantly.

He laughed. "Nothing like talking about relationships to make everybody back off."

"You're right there," she agreed, with a smile. "Also nobody wants to send anybody running."

"No, and I definitely don't want to send you running," he declared, with a bright smile. "What I would like is to see you by my side, as I move forward into this whole new venture. Knowing that you care about me, the person, and care on a level that sees us moving forward toward something permanent."

Her eyes widened, as she stared at him.

Wesley hesitated, but then he caught a glimpse of a tear in the corner of her eye. He wiped it off her face. "And I don't know what to think of that tear," he noted hesitantly, "but it definitely has me worried."

She shook her head. "No." She tried to smile through the tears that were even now running down her face. "No, it's all good," she said, "but I didn't think I would ever find anybody."

"And I'd had hoped to, but I was always holding back because you're somebody I work with all the time," he said. "Yet, because of that, I feel we've come further and faster in many ways than we would have in any other circumstances. But I also know that we could have a few issues going forward as, you know, I might tell you to butt out of my life every once in a while."

She burst out laughing. "And you know something? That would be quite healthy if you did," she murmured.

"So, again, it's, … it's hard to bare my soul, but I really … I've done so much, and I've come so far, to see something that I didn't even think was possible and yet was right in front of me. I just wanted you to know how I felt." She leaned across the front seat and laid her head against his chest. He wrapped his good arm around her and held her close. "It would mean living with somebody with only one arm," he pointed out.

She looked up, her eyes twinkling. "And that's been a bother so far, hasn't it?" she quipped.

He laughed. "No, but there will be times that you could be embarrassed because I fall over something or I fall because my leg goes out from under me or—"

She placed her finger against his lips. "And there could be times when you are embarrassed by me," she added, "when I might fall because I'm not paying attention or my heel breaks or I just trip for no reason or I slip on water. Plus there's no guarantee that tomorrow I will be as physically complete as I am today," she added. "I see people like you day in and day out, and it's never been something that's ever bothered me. Maybe working at Hathaway is good for people like me because we come to terms with your injuries faster than you guys do. However, it still has to be something that you're comfortable with. It has to be something that you can do on your own and can feel fulfilled in a way that maybe we can help you with," she murmured.

He nodded. "And I have seen that time and again at Hathaway," he said, with a smile. "And I have to tell you that I think the best thing I ever did was come here. Not only did it help me to get back on my feet, but you helped me to get back into my own personality, into my own skin, in a way I didn't think possible," he murmured. "But more than that," he added, "I have a future. I have a life ahead of me now that I didn't even think was something that I could even look at in the same way. And it's all because of you."

She shook her head. "No, and again we're going back to that."

"I'm not saying this because I'm grateful," he clarified, "although, believe me, I am grateful. And I understand that you'll tell me it's because of me, and, yes, I'm the one who came to Hathaway, and I did the work," he admitted, "but it's been a special journey because of you, and I don't want it to end."

She looked at him, and her heart was in her eyes.

He continued. "So I don't even know if it's too early to say this because I feel as if I'm out of sync with everything else in life," he said, "but I wanted you to know that I think you're a very special person and that I'm not sure where or how it happened, but I fell in love with you somewhere along this pathway," he shared. "I just would really appreciate knowing if you felt the same way."

He stared intently into her eyes and what he saw made his heart loosen and his chest widen to hold his own heart, as it swelled up with joy. "You do, don't you?"

She sniffled and nodded. "Yes, absolutely. Absolutely, yes."

"So is this like maybe a done deal?" he asked.

"Is *what* a done deal?" she asked in a teasing tone.

He hesitated for a second, then asked, "Would you marry me? Alba, would you spend the rest of your life telling me when I should be a better person and standing by my side when I am that better person and being there when I wake up and I'm not a better person?" he asked, his lips twitching. "Because there'll be those days."

She reached up a hand, stroked his cheek, and asked him, "And you? Will you be there when I'm not a better person, on the days that I need to be told to be a better person?" She added, "Will you be there when I have an accident, if I have one, and I need somebody else to hold my hand and to tell me that it'll be okay because you already know that it'll be okay?"

He nodded. "Absolutely, it would be my honor."

And she whispered right back at him, "Ditto. The answer is yes, I would love to marry you."

He threw his arm around her, crushed her against his chest, and held her close. He whispered against her ear, "I love you. … I think I fell in love with that that very first day I arrived at Hathway House. I saw you on that horse, your red hair glistening in the sun, and I somehow knew. Yet I didn't think this would ever happen. And to know that such a special person could fall in love with me? It's wondrous."

Immediately she placed a finger against his lips and whispered, "Right back at you."

He laughed and looked down at her huge chocolate-colored eyes, smiled, and said, "I think we need a kiss. We need to seal this deal with a kiss."

And he tilted her chin up, lowered his head, and poured into her all the promise and longing of a future together that he'd never thought would happen, but right now he finally believed that miracles were possible.

And he kissed her, for them, for tomorrow, and for every day thereafter.

Epilogue

THE ROOM WAS hot and airless with the windows closed, but, when you didn't have a private room and somebody else couldn't breathe in the cold air, you kept the window closed because it was the thing to do. But for his roommate's sake, Xavier would be outside, with that window open at all times. But it wasn't to be. He stared over at the man he had served with through many missions, not liking what he saw of his color. "Hey, do you want me to get you some help?"

Zander shook his head. "Nothing they can do, man." He turned to look at him and said, "I'm sure I got this virus here."

Xavier shrugged. "It would be hard not to, when it's going around."

"Yeah, well, before you get it, you should get out of here."

"I got no place to go," Xavier muttered.

"Find another center, find someplace where you could have the window open."

"You noticed that, *huh?*"

"Yeah, man. I'm sorry, but that cold air kills my lungs every time I inhale."

Xavier nodded. "That's why it's closed."

"And I appreciate it, yet you need to find another place

to stay."

"Yeah? Is there even another place?"

"A friend of mine went to Hathaway House," he shared, "and he swears by it."

"I've heard that a couple times too," Xavier noted, "but the whole process involved in leaving here sounds painful."

"I don't think it has to be," he said, and then he started to cough again.

Xavier winced. "Man, are you sure you don't want me to call somebody?"

"Nobody to call for this," he said. "It's why I'm telling you to get out."

"Yeah, but it's not as if what happened to you can't happen elsewhere."

"Right, but you know something? Sometimes it's things like this that make you decide to change."

"Sure, but you're the one who's sick, so maybe *you* should be getting out of here."

"I gotta get rid of this virus first. Don't want to spread it around. If I could get clearance, I would," he muttered.

Xavier looked at Zander, frowning. "You don't have to give up though."

"I'm not giving up," he stated, "although, man, I've come to that point a couple times."

"That's one of the reasons why I'm still kinda here."

"Don't do that. You can't throw your life away, waiting on me," he replied. "Honest to God, apply for Hathaway and if you get in, leave."

"I'll apply if you do," Xavier murmured.

Coughing and laughing at that, Zander replied, "They already turned me down."

He stared at his friend. "Why?"

"Too soon after surgery, too many adaptations still, they didn't have a bed, *blah, blah, blah*. They put me on a waitlist," he added, "but that's just a nice way of saying, *Sorry, no*."

"Well, if they're like that," Xavier noted, "then I don't want to go."

Then Zander looked at him and shook his head. "Don't do that. Don't cut off your nose to spite your face," he pointed out. "You need this, and they can help you. If I had a chance of going, I would, and I would make the best I could out of it. … Besides, if you go, you can always put in a good word for me."

Xavier frowned at his friend. "I don't want to leave you here," he stated bluntly.

"You'll have to, because staying here is not doing you any good."

Xavier argued, "We've been to battle together too many times for me to walk away now."

"Then step forward," Zander ordered. "Step forward and take one for the team."

He snorted at that. "You mean, take something good for the team? Yeah, that's not the way I operate."

"At this point in time I think you need to. And, if there is any chance of my getting there, then it won't hurt to at least have a reference from somebody who is there."

"Doesn't mean that they'll even accept me," Xavier stated. "Besides, if they turned you down, they would leave me hanging."

"And turning me down does not mean that they'll turn you down." Zander glared at him. "You need to try."

And, with that, Xavier gave in less-than-gracefully.

Giving it a try was a whole different story than giving in.

But he expected to receive an absolute and complete no. When he got an acceptance, although it wouldn't take effect for another couple months, he was stunned. He hated to even tell Zander. Yet Zander was thrilled.

"Good, and I'm starting to feel much better too. The last dose of antibiotics helped."

"Well, getting your lung punctured and catching pneumonia at the same time, being on a ventilator too …"

"But I am slowly recovering, and that's what's given me hope," Zander declared.

"I still think I should stay though."

"No," he snapped. "You need to go." He glared at his friend. "Sometimes you have to walk alone."

"Walking alone isn't a problem," Xavier snapped, "but I don't like walking away from anybody."

"I'm not asking you to walk away," Zander murmured. "I'm asking you to go there first, to do your reconnaissance, and to report back."

At that, Xavier burst out laughing. "Okay, I can do that, but only if you promise that you will contact them every week, saying you're still looking to come. And, I mean, every week from now on, until I tell you to stop or until you hear from them that you're accepted."

"Do you think it will make any difference?" he asked doubtfully. "Won't that just piss them off?"

"Then piss them off," Xavier said. "At least it shows that you care and that you'll do everything it takes to get there. And I'll push from my side too."

"Yeah, don't you do anything to jeopardize your healing," he warned.

"I won't, but no way will I do well and not give you the exact same opportunity," Xavier declared. "Remember that."

Zander looked at him and smiled. "I'll remember it, but—just as much as I'll email them every week—I will email you and give you a virtual kick in the butt to make sure you do the best you can there."

"While I'm there, you know it. But I'll be pissed if you can't come and join me."

"Don't hold it against them," Zander warned. "They must have rules, regulations, and limited places for people."

"Good, depending on how long it takes, we'll make sure there's a spot for you, so you sit tight. You're coming, whether you like it or not."

"You know I want to go," Zander said. Then he started another horrific set of coughing. But at least it seemed productive, moving around some of the congestion. And when he stared back over at Xavier, Zander smiled and said, "I really am feeling better."

"Yeah, *sure*," Xavier said in disgust.

"You need to leave before you catch something that'll kill you."

"Same for you," he muttered. "Same for you."

And, with that, he settled down to rest, wondering what the odds were of getting Zander into the Hathaway place while Xavier was still there. Probably not all that great odds, but he would do whatever he could. Zander had saved his life. If Xavier could return the favor now, he was up for it. In fact, he was bound and determined to do it, whether his friend liked it or not.

This concludes Book 23 of Hathaway House: Wesley.
Read about Xavier: Hathaway House, Book 24

Hathaway House: Xavier
(Book #24)

Welcome to Hathaway House. Rehab Center. Safe Haven. Second chance at life and love.

Self-sabotage isn't a concept Xavier is familiar with, until he ends up at Hathaway House—his application sent in with his buddy's. When Xavier's application was accepted, but his friend's wasn't, Xavier struggles with success. Even his arrival at Hathaway is bittersweet, knowing his friend has been rushed back to the hospital.

Talia, a patient coordinator at Hathaway House, witnesses Xavier's arrival, her heart tugging at his obvious sense of guilt. Even with Xavier's stomach barely holding down food and with his mind and soul emotionally struggling without his buddy, she knows Xavier's got what it takes to make a great recovery here—if he just focuses on his own life.

Hathaway is about progress, as Xavier's about to find out, … with friends and without.

Find Book 24 here!

To find out more visit Dale Mayer's website.

https://geni.us/DMSXavier

Author's Note

Thank you for reading Wesley: Hathaway House, Book 23! If you enjoyed the book, please take a moment and leave a short review.

Dear reader,

I love to hear from readers, and you can contact me at my website: www.dalemayer.com or at my Facebook author page. To be informed of new releases and special offers, sign up for my newsletter or follow me on BookBub. And if you are interested in joining Dale Mayer's Reader Group, here is the Facebook sign up page.
http://geni.us/DaleMayerFBGroup

Cheers,
Dale Mayer

About the Author

Dale Mayer is a *USA Today* best-selling author, best known for her SEALs military romances, her Psychic Visions series, and her Lovely Lethal Garden cozy series. Her contemporary romances are raw and full of passion and emotion (Broken But … Mending, Hathaway House series). Her thrillers will keep you guessing (Kate Morgan, By Death series), and her romantic comedies will keep you giggling (*It's a Dog's Life*, a stand-alone novella; and the Broken Protocols series, starring Charming Marvin, the cat).

Dale honors the stories that come to her—and some of them are crazy, break all the rules and cross multiple genres!

To go with her fiction, she also writes nonfiction in many different fields, with books available on résumé writing, companion gardening, and the US mortgage system. All her books are available in print and ebook format.

Connect with Dale Mayer Online

Dale's Website – www.dalemayer.com
Twitter – @DaleMayer
Facebook Page – geni.us/DaleMayerFBFanPage
Facebook Group – geni.us/DaleMayerFBGroup
BookBub – geni.us/DaleMayerBookbub
Instagram – geni.us/DaleMayerInstagram
Goodreads – geni.us/DaleMayerGoodreads
Newsletter – geni.us/DaleNews